WEST

BILLIONAIRE RANCH - 4

VANESSA VALE

GET A FREE VANESSA VALE BOOK!

Join Vanessa's mailing list to be the first to know of new releases, free books, special prices and other author giveaways.

http://freeromanceread.com

1

EST

Turned out, Rory Sullivan, the New York lawyer who'd been waiting at the airport, was not a guy. And she had the prettiest nipples I'd ever seen. How the hell did I know that? Because I was eyeing them, watching as they hardened in the cool air of her hotel room.

"You going to look or are you going to touch?" she asked, reaching up and taking off my Stetson. She tossed it somewhere behind me as I continued to take in those hard tips.

Fuck if that ballsy question didn't make my dick hard. *Harder.*

I had one hand braced on the door above her head. I was close, but not touching. We hadn't made it any further into the room before I spun her to face the door, slid the zipper down the back of her high-powered dress and pushed it down to her hips. Next went the catch on her bra and when I turned her back around, it fell right off.

She was a tiny thing and my head was tilted down to take her all in, but I lifted my gaze from her spectacular rack to her green eyes.

"You going to stop with the sass or am I going to have to make you?" I asked.

Her eyes flared with a mixture of determination, fury and need at my question.

This hate/fuck banter had been going on since baggage claim. She'd come to Montana a day early for a meeting at Wainright Holdings but had decided a ride on a cowboy's dick was a way to kick the trip off.

I was more than happy to oblige, as long as it was mine she was climbing on.

I'd figured her out pretty quickly. Walking into the baggage area I'd found the New Yorker my sister, North, asked me to collect and entertain. Except she hadn't been a guy. *She'd* been in a slim cut dress that screamed big city. It had a conservative cut meant for a Connecticut country club filled with stodgy rich folk, except it showed off every curve of her pint-sized body. If that wasn't enough, she wore a pair of ruthless heels that did plenty for her legs. It had been the phone connected to her head like a teenager and the way her toe tapped on the industrial carpet that clinched my thoughts about her.

Rory Sullivan, the sexy as fuck power broker, was a wound tight, sexy siren who'd made my dick hard from across the luggage conveyor belt. I'd instantly wanted to fuck the high-maintenance, East coast workaholic, who, by the half of the conversation I'd been able to overhear, probably wore a string of weak men's balls as a necklace.

Maybe that had been it, her *I'm in fucking charge* attitude that was so out of place here in Big Sky country. I wanted to bend her to my will. Get her on her knees. Fuck that priss right out of her. Make her forget the names of her clients as well as her own.

To *rule* her world.

I'd gone to the airport in the first place because my sister had discovered I was in town to do my monthly big-box store shopping and had asked. I spent my days in the saddle and no doubt she wanted me to have a conversation with a real person instead of a horse. She was worried about me now that she—a ball buster herself—had found Jed Barnett.

North didn't have to worry. Fuck, no. I could deal with people when I wanted. One sexy one in particular, especially naked.

I doubted North envisioned this kind of *Welcome to Montana* from me, but she sure as shit couldn't complain I wasn't being attentive. I'd headed us toward my favorite burger restaurant, intending to feed Rory dinner and drop her off at her hotel. Instead, she'd said she wanted a different kind of meat... no, she hadn't said that exactly. But something else just as bold that'd had me turning my truck toward her hotel and instead of leaving her at the entrance, escorted her to her room.

And out of her bra.

Rory's small hands went to my belt buckle as she eyed me. Tipped her chin up when she reached in and—

I hissed at the aggressive tug. "You might have your hand around my dick," I told her, leaning down to kiss those sassy lips. She moaned and I took the kiss deep. I tangled my fingers in her long hair. Pulled a little when she gave me a rough stroke. "But if you think you're in charge..."

I couldn't say much more than that, because *fuck*

me her hand felt good. Her grip was firm as it slid up and down the shaft. The swipe of her thumb over the tip was like heaven. I was going to come like a guy who hadn't fucked in a while.

I'd assumed I was too old for the stranger-fucking routine, but she'd changed my mind. I *was* content about this one-off. I didn't do more, especially with a woman from the East coast. I'd dated—and fallen for —one in college, wanted more and gotten burned. Not fucking happening again.

"You sure about that?" she replied, sounding pretty happy with bringing a six-four man to his knees.

Because I did just that, dropped to my knees on the rug in front of her, tugged the dress down her hips and it pooled around her ankles. She kicked it free and there she was, a little firecracker in ruthless stilettos and a black lace thong.

The corner of my mouth tipped up. "That wet spot makes me feel pretty confident."

I ran a knuckle over the damp gusset and she sucked in a breath.

She was so fucking pretty. Flushed and silky soft, sweet scented and... I slid that scrap of fabric to the side, leaned in and licked up her seam. Yeah, she tasted sweet too.

"I'm always in charge," she breathed, then gave a little whimper.

"Why are you here, half pint?" I wanted to see how long she could hold a conversation while I was licking her pussy.

"Montana? Or with you?"

"Both."

"I close this deal, I make partner. As for you—" She actually shrugged. "—you're hot and you're probably better than the vibrator I've got in my suitcase."

My dick punched against my jeans at the thought of her in bed, legs parted and working herself with vibrating silicone. I pushed aside the thoughts of her ruthless focus on the corner office.

"Something this pretty needs more than hardware," I said, then licked her again. "Montana's a little out of your comfort zone. No skyscrapers or weak men to crush beneath those heels. So you want to feel back in charge, getting me to come to your room. Use me for your orgasms."

Her eyes flared and she blushed.

Her clit was swollen and shiny and I ran the tip of my tongue around it.

"I'm fine with the last. Hell, I'm on my knees. But I run this show." I screwed a finger into her dripping pussy. Fuck, she was tight.

"Weston," she breathed.

If she didn't believe me, I was going to prove it to her.

Then her cell rang.

I pulled back, ran my tongue over my lips. I hadn't even realized she still had her phone in her hand, as if it was glued to it.

Looking up at her, I arched a brow. "You gonna answer that while I eat your pussy?"

She looked at me with a blurry gaze, then at the screen. Then back at me. "I need to–"

"Come all over my face," I finished for her. Yeah, if she was considering answering a work call now, I sure as shit had my work cut out for me.

"I'm here for work."

"Yeah, I got that. Corner office. The meeting's tomorrow, half pint."

"You wouldn't understand," she countered, the cell still ringing.

"Because I don't have a college degree or because I ride a horse for work instead of the subway?" All she knew was that a Wainright ranch hand was to pick her up. Not a Wainright himself. I didn't lie about my name back at the airport, but I was technically a fucking ranch hand. Except I ran my own ranch. I wore the hat.

The jeans. The big belt buckle. If the snap shirt fit...

She was a lawyer, here for a meeting with the legal team at corporate. I didn't ask her details about whatever contract or legal paperwork they were going to review because I didn't give a shit about the family business. North ran that show. I'd wanted no part in it, when Macon had been alive and even now.

"Don't lose your nerve now, half pint," I told her. "You might have to work, but this takes multitasking to a whole new level."

Her eyes narrowed, as if I'd insulted her. As if giving in to me meant she gave up in general. She raised her phone, swiped the screen then brought it to her ear as if more to fuck with me than anything else.

"Mike."

Mike?

I was taking in the perks of a quality pussy waxing while she talked to another man.

"Yes, I'm aware of the issue with the clause and am prepared." She looked at me as she spoke.

Game. Fucking. On.

If this was how she wanted me to eat her out, talking to some asshole named Mike, then fine. I would have taken my time with her pussy, settled in for a while, but hell no. I was getting this woman off like it was my job.

Her thong was so skimpy, it took one tug to rip it away. The scrap slid down around her right ankle. Hooking her leg, I tossed it over my shoulder and went to work. Her pussy was dripping, hot and fucking perfect.

"Yes," she said, talking to the man on the phone but the roll of her hips indicated it might have been for me.

One of my hands cupped her ass, the other slid up the inside of her thigh, smearing her arousal over my palm. With my mouth on her clit, I slipped a finger—a big, ranch hand callused finger—into her tight pussy and curled it. Her hips rolled as if she were reaching for that orgasm.

Her angry gaze hazed and she whimpered.

I could hear a voice through the phone but not the words. I couldn't help but smirk.

"You'll have to figure it out on your own. I have something urgent here," she said, although her voice was more lusty than legal. "Yes. No. Yes."

She came while on a fucking work call, her pussy clenching and milking my finger, her eagerness for more dripping down to my palm as her little clit swelled and pulsed beneath my tongue. Her heel against my back dug in.

Her arm fell to her side as if she couldn't hold it up. I pulled back to take it from her, made sure that call was done. My finger was still inside her, still rubbing that spot that had her hips rolling and her eyes falling closed.

I didn't want to tear my gaze away from watching her give over, because she was fucking incredible like this, but I had to power that fucking phone down and toss it over my shoulder—the one that didn't have her knee bent over it.

"Here's how this is going to go," I told her. I licked my lips and savored that sticky honey. "You're going to come again as you sit on my face. Then bend over the bed and take my dick nice and deep. Those stilts can stay on, but that's the last time you'll think about a fucker named Mike. Or work. Or anything but how my dick's going to fill you up. The only name you'll say for the next few hours is mine. You'll go to that meeting tomorrow, prepared like I'm sure you already fucking are, with a sore pussy as a reminder that you might be the boss in the boardroom, but when you're with me, you give over."

She nodded.

"I need to hear the words, half pint. Say, '*Yes, Weston.*'"

I may have pushed, but I had a feeling this woman needed someone to take charge, even for a little bit. Here, in a hotel room in Montana, two time zones away from her real life, was a safe place to do just that.

"Yes, Weston."

"Good girl."

Yeah, she was different like this. All soft and pliant. Sated and flushed. I meant what I said. An over-worked, wound tight woman who needed to wind that shit down and get out of her head? I was the man for the job. It was a role I never knew I ever wanted and that was a fucking problem.

2

ORY

"MONTANA?" my mother asked.

"Yes, I'm in Montana." I stood in the hallway outside the restrooms on the second floor of Wainright Holdings corporate office. Before the meeting wasn't the best time to take her call, but she'd keep at it if I didn't. Taking a moment now would allow me to focus on one less thing.

"Whyever would you want to go there? Isn't it dangerous? All cows and gunslingers?"

She sounded horrified and that made me laugh. Although it was her ignorance that made it come out brittle. "I haven't seen a cow yet and we live in New York City. There are probably more gunslingers in lower Manhattan."

She sighed and I could imagine her playing with the pearls she always had around her neck. "Still, dear. I have no idea why you keep up with this... dream of yours."

"To be a partner in the family law firm? You know the answer." We had this conversation at least once a month and it had been going on since I decided to become a lawyer instead of marrying one.

"You don't need to do any of that. I'm leaving now to meet Alice Dunsford for facials and blowouts before dinner at Chez Manu. All this organizing for the gala is making my skin tired."

"I'm sorry to hear about your skin." I wasn't, but it was easier to placate her. Eleanor Duffield Sullivan hadn't worked a day in her life and went to college to get her Mrs. degree. She spent my father's money lavishly while he worked constantly, most likely to see her as little as possible. It was a match made in society heaven. "I have to go, Mother. My meeting's about to start."

"You'll be back for the gala?"

"Of course," I replied. I could put her off, but not the gala.

"Mark Rutherford will be there. I spoke with his mother yesterday at—"

"I'm not interested in Mark."

I thought of a specific rugged cowboy I'd kicked out of my hotel room the night before and wondered if Mark could fuck like Weston. The answer was a definite no.

"Goodbye, Mother."

I hung up, resolving one problem. I turned on my patent stiletto and made my way to the conference room.

"What the hell was up with you yesterday?"

I glanced up from my stack of papers at the question not a minute later. Mike pulled out the chair beside me and dropped into it. He was another associate at the firm, one who was destined to... make my face go dry.

He didn't wait for a reply, just plowed on. "You cut our talk about clause twelve short, then you don't answer all night?" He leaned in and fixed his dark eyes on mine. "Are you even prepared for this?"

I bristled. I was *always* prepared and the fact that he questioned that pissed me off.

"First off, if you need me to hand hold you through clause twelve, then you're the one who isn't prepared."

I thought of the call and how Weston had licked

my pussy while Mike had droned on in my ear. It was almost impossible not to squirm in the conference room chair remembering. The cowboy had been a man of his word and done every single thing he'd said. And more.

I hadn't kicked him out until after ten, and I didn't mean the number of orgasms he'd given me. I'd worked late into the night, going over the details of the pending contract. I knew them all, but I was a perfectionist. I also couldn't fuck up, not even the smallest amount because Mike would swoop in like a vulture and finish me off, ensuring the latest partner spot was his instead of mine.

"I also want to know why you kept trying to call me all night," I countered. "I'm not your mother."

The fact that he made me even think that was how much I didn't like the guy. We'd gone out on one date. One. And it hadn't really been a date. Drinks after work. He'd probably assumed it would have led to him being in my bed, but it hadn't. God, no. Michael Spain didn't like to be denied. Whether it was a win in the courtroom or with a woman. So he'd hated me ever since.

I regretted the one glass of wine even more than the *Cinco de Mayo* event at my sorority house sophomore year of undergrad. Mike would do anything to make partner, including fucking me and using it against me. He'd stoop to any advantage because he thought I had one, the fact that my father was a founder of the law firm where we worked. While my last name was on the company business card, it wasn't *me* it referenced. I didn't have a penis, which seemed to be my biggest weakness because no matter what I did, how hard I worked, how many cases I actually won, I still didn't make my father happy.

I'd get that partnership instead of Mike. Every hour of my day was focused on it.

"We can't leave this state without the papers signed," he said. "This deal is important to Nixon, Sullivan and Proctor." I could hear my father's voice in Mike's words.

I'd learned long ago not to let my emotions show. It was a weakness as a lawyer, but it went back so much farther than that, to being the little sister to Matthew, the perfect Sullivan firstborn and now renowned neurosurgeon. And male. Any emotion, whether it be too much pleasure in something, frustration or even crying, had been shamed out of me.

Oh, Rory. Can't you be like Matthew? Such a little girl, crying like that. A ninety-three? That's the best you could get? Be a little lady and get your nails done with your mother for the pool party.

"Thank you for reminding me," I said neutrally, looking away from him and back on my papers. I didn't need to organize them as I knew exactly the order they were in, but I didn't want to listen to Mike drone on about how lacking I was.

My thoughts drifted to Weston because based on the way his dick had stayed hard after coming not once, but twice, he was the only guy I knew who found me anything but lacking.

It had been crazy. While I was assertive in the courtroom, propositioning a sexy cowboy was not something I normally did. I *never* did it. Maybe it was the fact that Montana was nowhere near New York. What I did in a Billings hotel room couldn't be used against me.

Especially since I'd *let* him be in charge. Mike mansplained everything. Told me how to do my job and even tried to finagle me into doing his.

I never let my guard down. Never ceded control of anything to anyone. Ever.

Except with his bossy tone and skilled tongue, I'd let Weston take charge. Yeah, *let.*

And... I'd liked it.

Loved it.

He hadn't mansplained. He'd just been a *man.* Maybe that was what drew me to him. He had muscles honed from hard work, not made from a standing appointment with a personal trainer. He took charge. Made me feel small. Feminine, and that was a positive to him. Not something to loom over me as a weakness.

It had been amazing until I let reality sneak in and made me question my sanity for taking a few hours off in the first place. I'd tossed him his jeans and thanked him for the orgasms. When the door shut behind him and his satisfied smirk, relieved I'd never see that sexy ass again, I got back to my regularly scheduled life. Like this important meeting with North Wainright herself.

"I assume Nate and Paul have your answers at the ready."

The two men who flew in with Mike settled beside him, pulling out their laptops and focusing solely on work. As paralegals, they were sidekicks only to Mike's superhero status at this meeting. They'd get no credit, offered no purpose other than to make him shine.

They were technically here for me as well, but I never relied on someone else like Mike did. I worried they'd screw with me to see me stumble and fall, but it took more than a bump in the road to make me trip in my heels. I'd learned that once the first year as an associate. Since then, I worked extra hours to ensure I didn't have to rely on anyone.

Mike said something under his breath and turned his attention away from me.

Sure, I'd flown in early to prep, but also because I hadn't wanted to travel with Mike. The fact that we had to work closely was torture enough.

Before he could condescend to me any further, the conference room doors opened. I stood and faced North Wainright. There was no question she was the CEO.

I'd spoken to her several times on the phone and felt we'd connected, at least as much as any business relationship could when we'd never met and only made nominal small talk, but her... power didn't come through the phone like it did with her in person.

For growing up on a ranch in Montana—albeit the largest one in the state—she looked nothing like a cowgirl. She wore a green dress and heels that were perhaps higher than my own. Her blonde hair was pulled back in a low bun at her nape and her makeup was simple but impeccable. Everything about her screamed billionaire and she'd fit in perfectly in New York. It was the smile that she gave to me that hinted at the person beneath the CEO.

"Rory. It's nice to finally put a face with a voice," she said, coming to stand before me.

"Likewise," I said, shaking her hand.

An entourage entered, fanning out on both sides of her. One man and four women. Her legal team, I assumed.

"I'm Michael Spain." Mike practically bumped me out of the way to get in front of her. "I must say, I haven't met a prettier CEO."

Fuck. Me. I kept my smile plastered on my face as North Wainright narrowed her eyes and *her* smile slipped.

"The last time I checked, Mr. Spain," she began, turning her back on him and making her way to the seat at the head of the table. "Harvard and Wharton didn't give out beauty sashes with their degrees."

Her employees settled across from us at the table, not interested in Mike's attempt at male humor.

Mike cleared his throat as his cheeks flushed. He sat down, clearly not used to dealing with a woman in charge.

I introduced Nate and Paul, then took my seat.

"I hope your arrival yesterday allowed for some free time," North began, offering me a smile. "Montana is quite different from New York."

The view out the window behind her was proof of that. No skyscrapers, only low buildings and in the distance grassy plains and mesas.

"Yes, thank you." There was no way in hell I was

going to say more than that. I didn't think telling her I fucked her ranch hand was a good idea. Like Weston had said, my pussy was as sore as he'd promised. "Shall we share with you the final draft of the contracts? I know how much our client wishes to use the patents."

She nodded and I opened my folder and handed a stack of documents to the Wainright lawyer across from me. She distributed them to the others, although I saw that they'd brought their own copies. I was pleased they were efficient and organized, a good indication of their investment in this meeting.

"Yes," North agreed. "I admit—and don't tell my brothers this—while one twin has a PhD in math, it's the other who's the smart one. He has six patents to date and I believe two more are pending."

While she was poking fun at her siblings, her tone and the look on her face spoke of her fondness for them. Love, even, which I didn't really understand when it came to a sibling. Matthew was my older brother, the annoying person whose shadow I'd had to live in. Hell, I still did.

As for the patents themselves, I was very familiar with the devices and micro-workings that were the basis for this meeting. I didn't understand exactly how they worked, the complex dynamics of the valves and parts, but I knew they were ingenious and well designed. Enough to be patented.

They belonged to North's brother and that while he'd done the hard work, he left it up to her to see to the business end of things.

"Impressive," I said, meaning it. We were here as representatives for a client, an engineering firm that wished to purchase the rights to several of the Wainright patents to use in their business. Nixon, Sullivan and Proctor were on retainer for their legal services, which included making the rights transfer legal. Meaning me. And Mike.

It meant a potential for millions for the engineering firm's profit margin. I knew it was a tidy sum for Wainright Holdings as well. And for me to clinch this contract, well, it meant the corner office. Plus, I didn't want to go back and listen to my father go off on how disappointed he was. *And* possibly pat Mike on the back and talk about new projects in the men's room where I never had access.

"My brother doesn't usually join us on patent negotiations, but I thought he might want to sit in on this one."

I cocked my head to the side. I was used to judges and opposing counsel changing things up so North's statement didn't faze me. "Your brother?"

She nodded. "He's not usually late, so I expect him to walk in at any time."

I cleared my throat and got focused. "Great, until then, we can go over a sticky spot. I know there was a question the other day about clause twelve—"

I didn't say more because the conference room doors opened.

"There he is," North said with a smile, standing.

I swiveled in my chair and faced—

"West," North called.

I stared at Weston the Ranch Hand and using those on-the-fly problem solving skills, I realized that he was actually *West Wainright*.

Holy. Fucking. Fuckety fuck.

Mike stood first and I pushed to my feet. Adrenaline coursed through me as my mind did a warp-speed recap of being pressed into the bed and being fucked hard and deep from behind while my hair was tugged and told to *take it*.

I stared at Weston. No, *West*. He didn't even look around, only homed in on me. His eyes widened, but he must have played a mean game of Poker because he, thankfully, didn't give any outward sign that he knew me.

"You said this was a patent meeting," he said, the

tip of his head the only indication that he was speaking to his sister. His sister, the fucking CEO!

Oh, that voice. The one that murmured in my ear as he did all kinds of naughty, wild things.

"It is," she countered.

"I know lawyers when I see them."

"This is the team from Nixon, Sullivan and Proctor. The legal team for the engineering company that's buying your rights."

West's dark brow rose sky high, then he took a step closer. Perhaps a touch too close, forcing me to tip my chin back to keep his gaze. "Weston Wainright."

Yeah, I finally got the actual introduction. The day before, he'd only shared his first name. His *full* first name. Nothing more. I'd never made the connection between Weston the Ranch Hand and West the Wainright billionaire. Maybe part of that was on me because every article about the family mentioned them by their nicknames, at least for the three brothers, South, East and West. When we'd been together, I hadn't asked him for specifics. I'd been more interested in his dick and oral skills than anything else about him.

That had been a mistake.

North had been the one to email and offered for a *ranch hand* to pick me up at the airport. Was she in on this? Had she intentionally left out who he was? No, I couldn't see the woman power-brokering her brother into bed with anyone.

I took a deep breath, thought of West as a difficult witness and prepared for what I'd come to Montana to achieve, and it wasn't multiple vaginal and clitoral orgasms. Not to mention the one where he'd had his thumb pressed to my—

I nodded my head, clearing that thought, then licked my suddenly dry lips. His eyes lowered to watch the motion. "Rory Sullivan. These are my associates, Nate, Paul and—"

"Michael Spain." Mike stuck out his hand, not waiting for me to introduce him.

The differences between the men were obvious. West was at least four inches taller and had thirty pounds of muscle on Mike. While Mike wore a bespoke suit that probably put a big dent in his associate-level salary all in the need to look *more,* West had on an outfit similar to the one he'd stripped off the day before, right down to the hat I'd flung from his head.

He looked *nothing* like a man who'd spent two years at MIT and single handedly changed the way water usage for grazing was handled in the West. I knew this—not from when he'd told me to suck his cock—but from reading articles on the man as part of my research. Articles that had no photos.

West took his time, but finally shook hands. "You go by Mike?" he asked.

"Yes."

A slow smile spread across West's face and he clapped once, cut around behind us and settled his super-sized frame into the chair at the foot of the table. He removed his hat. "Well, this is going to be good then."

Good? This was a nightmare. I slept with the client. More specifically, the actual patent holder himself. If anyone at work found out, they'd think I'd done it to get the partnership. Mike would point out that I hadn't been able to get it on merit, but on sexual talent.

This was a disaster. It was an issue of my making and I had no idea how to solve it.

3

 EST

MY SISTER rarely meddled in my life. When she did, it was a pain in my ass. I'd thought that was the case today when she'd *suggested* I attend the patent meeting with the lawyers. Long ago, we'd established a hands-off approach, where I did the inventing and she did the paperwork and deals. I wanted nothing to do with any of the corporate shit. As for the money the patents brought in? I had more than I could spend in my life-time. I didn't give a shit about more.

The ideas came to me and I tinkered and invented shit. Shit that was actually useful.

But that was *all*. I ranched. I puttered around in my workshop. After growing up with Macon—the man we'd all thought was our father until last year—I kept what I did to myself. It didn't matter that I got all A's in school. It didn't matter that I played varsity football as a freshman. Or went to MIT. Macon had *hated* anything that made the four of us happy. So I'd learned to tamp it all down and keep it to myself. To not stand out. Even excelling at something meant hearing his wrath. So I stopped giving a shit about anything, keeping its value to me low.

North had been fucked over the most, so she knew my issues. The fact that she was taking interest in my personal life was a surprise. When she said I should sit in on a meeting today about my patents, I grumbled all the way to the office. She didn't ask often, so what got me through the door was the *why* of the request. Why these patents? Why this week?

It was fucking obvious. I was smart enough to catch on to the matchmaking North was doing. *Now*. She hadn't told me Rory Sullivan was a woman when I'd gone to the airport. North hadn't told me this meeting included her, either. All I knew from Rory herself was she was here to meet with the Wainright lawyers, but not about my patents.

What I hadn't told North—or anyone—was that

I'd gotten the woman to scream my name as I took her hard. Not that I'd ever kiss and tell to my sister. Fuck, I knew she and Jed Barnett had sex, but I wouldn't let my mind linger there.

But matchmaking? North was insane because a New York City-based lawyer who probably hadn't ridden a horse or anything else before my dick? It was a good thing North was a skilled CEO because she had no fallback career in creating relationships.

I wasn't looking for one. Sure, all of my siblings had settled down over the past year. Maybe North wanted to see me in love, too. It was fine for them and all, but me?

I was satisfied with my life as it was and watching them squirm and suffer through the pain of falling for someone. None of them had gone down easy. Or without fucking danger.

Things were just the way I liked them. Calm.

From the look on Rory's face when I came in, she'd been as stunned as me. Yeah, she hadn't been expecting the patent creator to show up. Or be the guy who'd picked her up at the airport or who she'd propositioned.

I'd settled at the end of the table not to listen to the contract negotiations. I didn't give a shit about any of that.

No.

I wanted to know everything about this Mike character. Because just looking at him I knew he was a douche canoe. His nails were fucking manicured. His hair had more product in it than a pageant queen. I wanted to know about the man who Rory had felt obligated to talk to while her clit had been in my mouth.

It said something about his importance in her life. I just wasn't sure what that was. Yet.

"Now that introductions have been made," North began, then eyed me suspiciously. *Yeah, sis. This is exactly where you wanted me to be.* "Rory, would you like to start again?"

Everyone returned to their seats. Rory appeared like she had her shit together. Today she had on a crisp blue dress with short sleeves and a shiny black belt. Her shoes—again heels as ruthless as my sister's—were just as shiny. I had to wonder if I could tell the color of her panties in that sheen. But I'd seen her when she'd relaxed those shoulders, emptied that sharp mind and let go. Her hair had been a tangle instead of the currently sleek ponytail.

Right now, she was taking a moment to reorganize. I'd flustered her. My dick liked that, and while I loved that I was able to do it, messing with her focus during an important work meeting wasn't my intention. But she was all paperclips and schedules. Planners and details. A workaholic. She was exactly what I *didn't* want.

Fucking her was one thing, but thinking of anything more? Dumbest thing I'd considered in a long time. Since... Carrie.

The last thing I wanted, or needed, was a woman who chose her career over me. I'd had that back in college and I sure as shit wasn't going through that again. It had been bad enough having Macon be manipulative. I hadn't expected it from a girlfriend, a woman I'd taken to my bed and let into my heart, learning she'd been using her connections with a Wainright to advance her newfound career, then dumping me once she had what she wanted. Advancement.

Of course, I never expected to see Rory again after we both came a few times. She'd practically pushed me out her hotel room door. I barely had my shirt buttoned when it was shut in my face. My male pride hadn't been dented. Hell, no. It had been a sexy romp and knowing I'd tamed her had stroked it instead. I'd known the score going in that it was a one-off. I'd been relieved. She hadn't been a clinger. Far from needy. I hadn't had to slip out after she'd fallen asleep.

Rory'd made it crystal clear that she was working her ass off for this contract solely to land partner. This meeting was truly a business transaction for her. That was fine. I was sure North felt the same way. But last night, when I'd had Rory begging me to take her harder, deeper, faster, that hadn't been anything other than two consenting adults gaining mutual pleasure.

No feelings. No attachment.

So yeah, a one-night stand had been fine. Because the last thing I needed were feelings for a woman whose life was her career and didn't have room for anything else.

When she'd answered her cell as I ate her out proved how driven she was.

I'd thought that had been it. Hot sex. But now here Rory was and it seemed she'd been just as surprised to see me. As feisty and ruthless as ever and for some fucking reason I was pleased to see her. All I wanted to do—besides punch Mike in the face—was to find an empty office and fuck her over the desk. Get her to submit to me again.

I shifted my dick beneath the conference table and sat back to watch. This was Rory's element and I wanted to see her in it.

She gave North a brittle smile while picking up her

pen. "Sure. As I said, we can answer any questions you have about clause twelve."

"Mike, why don't you tell me about it?" I asked.

Heads swiveled my way in unison while I looked to the high-maintenance shithead. His spine went straight. So did Rory's beside him, probably assuming I wanted the man to take over.

"Of course." Mike cleared his throat and glanced down, realizing he didn't even have the contract in front of him. Paul, who sat to his left, slid his copy over. Mike flipped through. "Clause twelve references..." He paused as he searched.

Rory wasn't bailing him out, but Paul did, pointing to a spot halfway down the page.

"Right. Okay." He scanned it. Then again. "Rory?"

I leaned forward and set my forearms on the table. "Oh? You're not familiar with the contract? I'd think if you came this far you'd be prepared."

Mike blustered and turned a shade of red only seen in those about to have a stroke.

"I assure you," he sputtered. "The NSP team is here to resolve any issues with the contract until you are satisfied about signing on the dotted line."

"I only get the patents." I pointed down the long table. "My sister's the one who makes the deals."

All heads pivoted to North.

She gave Mike an unimpressed look that probably shriveled his balls. "Please continue, Rory."

Yeah, I'd made my point. That dickhead knew shit.

Rory jumped right in and gave a quick recap of clause twelve and then answered questions North and her legal team had, taking notes on her paper copy while it appeared Paul made changes directly to the document on his laptop.

I didn't say a word, only watched how sharp and talented Rory was. She'd been so wound up about being prepared, she'd flown in a day early. Probably stayed up to work more after she'd kicked me out. The effort paid off because the lawyers across from her were asking fewer questions.

North was going to sign, but when she looked at her watch, I knew it wasn't going to be today.

"It's time to stop for now." She looked to the New York crew. "You've had a long day of travel and my helicopter takes me home at five-thirty."

Jed had put constraints on her workaholic ways. Now she ended her day at a reasonable hour. North was the boss of a billion-dollar company, but in her relationship with Jed, she deferred to him. Not because she was less, but because it somehow worked. She knew she needed the boundaries he'd helped her set and she was happier for it. If she wasn't, he'd be dead and buried where no one could find him, even his former employer, the FBI.

"We are prepared to stay late and finalize this," Mike told her. "That's why we're here."

"No," North replied. "We, as in me and Miss Sullivan, can start again in the morning." She stood and looked to Mike. "Gentlemen, you're dismissed. Thank you for coming to Montana, but I'll be handling the rest of the deal over the weekend."

Rory's mouth fell open, but she quickly snapped it shut. "Oh, that's kind of you but—"

"I don't think—" Mike sputtered at the same time.

North held up a hand as she looked at her watch once again. "Consider it Montana hospitality, Rory. Besides, it's not often I get to have girl talk. Lots of men in my family." She gave me a pointed stare. "The helicopter leaves in fifteen minutes. I'll see you on it."

Rory at the family ranch. For the weekend. I should hate the idea. I should be eager to see her on the first flight east. We'd both had our fun, but now that North—for some fucking reason—had pretty much forced her into staying, I was pretty happy about it. Yeah, that was stupid of me because this deal was done. Other than North signing, I wasn't sure what else there was to go over. The amount of money Wainright Holdings was going to make was astronomical. I hadn't even considered how desirable my patents were. Or how hard North pushed for them to be the most useful to the world—and lucrative.

But to keep Rory here? Was it meant as punishment? I couldn't see how a workaholic New Yorker would find being stuck on a ranch in Montana for the weekend enjoyable. Maybe North saw something of herself in Rory.

Whatever the reason, I had another opportunity to be with her even though come Monday morning she'd be on a plane, signed contract in hand, headed right for that shiny new partner desk.

Maybe North was right and I hadn't realized how eager I was for human interaction. Or maybe I was hooked on Rory's perfect pussy. Fuck if I knew why I wanted to put up with that sass. A meek, docile—*local* —woman would've been better. One who knew which end of a horse was front. Except that sounded boring as hell.

A weekend of Rory at the ranch. Stuck there. No subways or taxis to rescue her. Hell, yeah. I was going to make the most of it while it lasted.

 ORY

I HAD SO much work to do. I didn't have time to spend the weekend with North Wainright. I had to review the updated contract that Paul had emailed me, ensuring everything that had been discussed in the meeting was included, or removed. I had three other cases on hold while I was away and other issues that had filled my inbox over the past few hours. I'd expected the contract to be signed and my butt on a flight back to New York right now.

Instead, I'd taken a freaking helicopter to Billion-aire Ranch. And I'd had to make small talk with North and her boyfriend, Jed. I knew of him from my research, that he'd gone from the FBI to being the company's head of security. North hadn't been kidding about the five-thirty departure from the office. Jed had been waiting on the roof and eyeing his watch when we'd joined him. I'd felt like he was a middle school gym teacher clocking everyone on a one-mile run. Except Jed looked nothing like a gym teacher and the kiss he'd given North as he snagged her cell phone had been more R rated than PG.

The gesture—stealing the phone—was *very* familiar and only riled me up. Okay, their kiss had, too.

Maybe it was an alpha Montana male thing. Again, the phone theft *and* the thorough kiss because no one in New York had ever thought to take my phone or kiss the hell out of me. North hadn't seemed to care Jed had yanked away her lifeline like I had when West had taken mine. In fact, North didn't speak at all about the contract or patents on our flight, only asking after life in New York and where I'd gotten my shoes. It seemed we both liked high heels.

She'd literally left work behind, which I didn't understand at all. She was a savvy businesswoman at the helm of a billion-dollar company. Things could go wrong if she was out of touch. People might need answers. Forms left unsigned. Someone might want her job, although Jed probably had her back on that one.

I didn't have a Jed in my life or a leadership position. Yet. This contract was to have been simple. Fly in, have a meeting. Get the deal done. Fly home. Move into the corner office.

No. I was in the freaking middle of nowhere. I had no idea how to get back to town since I'd arrived by *helicopter.* It wasn't like I was camping in a tent with Boy Scouts though. This place was incredible. I could see why it was nicknamed Billionaire Ranch. It was a mansion that was a mix of old west and modern. Looking out the window, all I could see was open prairie and mountains in the distance.

Grass. Bugs. Wild animals. The wildest animal I came across in New York was Cammie, my mother's five-pound Pomeranian that had a full-time dog walker on staff.

After we landed, North had led me through the first floor and into an office. She assured me that someone would collect my things from the hotel and bring them here, then left me to change out of her work clothes.

That had been thirty minutes earlier and I hadn't seen her since. I paced in front of a huge antique desk, bookshelves surrounding me listening to my father. He'd called because Mike had—of course—tattled to him.

"This deal was to be closed," he said.

"I'm well aware of that, however North has not declined the contract, only wants to talk further."

"Then why didn't she stay and talk further? Why draw this out?"

I did wonder that too. The meeting had been later in the day to accommodate travel, but not being flexible in her end-of-work time was odd. She was the one we needed to sign, so no matter how eccentric this arrangement seemed, I didn't have a choice. And neither did my father.

"I was invited to spend the weekend by North Wainright herself. I'm surprised Mike left that part out."

Yeah, I sounded petty, as if I'd been squabbling with a sibling. But I didn't put it past Mike to spin what was going on in a way that made me look bad.

"He didn't," my dad replied in his usual curt tone. "But he's on his way back to the city now and you're—"

"What, Dad? I'm what?" I didn't know what he wanted from me. I was closing the deal. I was literally in the middle of nowhere because a client forced me into it. "You think I want to stay in Montana?"

"Just don't get sidetracked."

I looked out the window to the expansive Wainright property and gave a laugh, waved my hand in the air even though he couldn't see. "There is literally nothing here to sidetrack me."

Except there was. A big, burly cowboy who knew how to make me come faster and harder than anyone before. Or probably after. No. It had been a one-time thing and clearly been a mistake. A secret I had to keep.

"You know what's at stake with this deal," he reminded.

Yeah. Partner. The fact that he held it out there like a carrot dangling from a stick pissed me off.

He hung up without saying goodbye. I took a moment to calm down, knew it was impossible where my father was concerned. It was all work, all the time.

And that prompted me to the conference call I was supposed to be on. I looked up the info for it on my laptop and dialed in. Set my cell to speaker mode and half listened while working on the injunction for a different client that had to be filed on Monday. My feet were killing me so I pulled my heels off and sighed as I curled my toes into the Oriental rug.

I tried not to think about West. About how he was obviously a player. A billionaire player dressed up as a cowboy. Gorgeous, sexually skilled and well endowed.

He wasn't just a ranch hand having a little fling. No, he was West Wainright! Billionaire. Genius inventor. Sneak. *Player.*

I was fine and all with having a good time with a ranch hand, but how dare he trick me by not sharing his name. Did he have any idea the situation he'd put me in? And then showing up at the meeting? With Mike there? Thankfully, he hadn't let on we'd met before and I sure as shit wasn't going to tell anyone. Because if Mike found out? God, it would ruin every bit of work I'd put in since the beginning of law school when I'd started interning at the office. All that effort, all those years to get to partner and it could all be blown if the secret came out.

Paul and Nate wouldn't say a word if they figured it out. Hell, I'd barely heard them speak. Ever. But Mike? *Fuck.*

Having West at the meeting was actual proof of how stupid I'd been.

A travel fling. What happened in Vegas and all that. I'd thought, hot guy, what the hell? An hour of fun. But no. No! I picked the one man in the entire state who was all kinds of trouble. Life altering trouble and I didn't mean by how incredible the orgasms had been.

"It's nine in New York. People still have meetings? Don't you guys ever stop?"

I gasped and spun around. Speak of the fucking devil. West was in the doorway, arms crossed over his chest. He practically filled the space. Why did I have to hate someone who was just so gorgeous and dick-talented?

A dog nudged his leg and trotted in to say hi. I ran my hand over his—or her—soft fur before the dog snuck under the desk and flopped down. I was totally jealous of the animal's carefree life.

I tipped up my chin and shifted my arms to mimic West. "I'm expected to bill seventy-five hours a week."

His eyes went wide. "Are you serious?"

I arched a brow and he sighed.

"Of course, you are. Hang up, half pint."

"Stop calling me that and stop bossing me around," I snapped.

The voices on the call droned on in the background.

"You seemed to like it yesterday."

I strode over to him, yanked him into the room and shut the door behind him. "Jesus, keep your voice down!"

He laughed. Actually laughed! "I don't care what other people think. Besides, I might not live here anymore, but this is my house too."

"I'm not an actual guest. I'm representing a client. I'm *work*."

"Exactly," he countered. "You can bill every hour you're here. You're supposed to satisfy the Wainrights, I assume."

I narrowed my eyes. "You're perverted."

He laughed again. "My mind wasn't in the gutter like yours, but I like a woman who knows what she wants."

If smoke could come out of my ears, it would be now.

"Are you kidding me?" I asked, tossing up my hands. "Are you trying to ruin my life?"

He leaned down. "I'm trying to get you under me again."

Yeah, total player.

"You're the client, Weston!" I flung my arms in the air, then settled them on my hips. "Oh, I mean, *West*. The patent holder, no less."

He shrugged. "So? You didn't have an issue with it yesterday."

"I didn't know who you were yesterday." He was standing close enough that I poked him in the chest and all it did was remind me about how hard he was. How rugged. *Male.* "Why didn't you tell me? Is this what you do, fuck with people?"

Tucking his finger beneath my chin, he forced me to look at him. Since I had no shoes on, it was a long way up. His gaze was serious beneath the brim of his Stetson. "I fuck *you.* I didn't know who you were either. Hell, when North asked me to collect you, I thought you were a man."

I'd had that assumption made before. "Still, you slept with a client."

He shook his head. "I slept with an out-of-state lawyer."

"Semantics," I snipped.

"You're the lawyer. Details count."

I narrowed my eyes again and made a solid effort to unman him with a glare.

"What's the problem, half pint?" He asked. "We're consenting adults. You propositioned me."

"You're an asshole," I replied, turning my head to the side to get away from his heated touch.

He sighed. "Okay, maybe that was the wrong thing to say. The way you're looking at me I'm thinking you're going to murder my ass with one of your stilettos. The chef's made an egg casserole and I'm hungry. I love breakfast for dinner."

"Seriously? You're thinking about food?" How could he be so... so blasé about all this? Because his job wasn't on the line. He was a billionaire. He didn't have to work.

"I always think about food," he said. "But woman, what I meant was, you wanted something from me yesterday and was assertive enough to go after it. I like that."

He put his hand to the front of his jeans and actually shifted his dick. His hard dick pressing snugly against the fly. He moved close again, set his hand on my shoulder. "I also like the way you give over. It takes a little warming up, but you get there."

I could feel my cheeks heat. "So what, you want to sleep with me while I'm at your sister's house? A little extra fun before I go back to New York?"

"You're the one getting the corner office out of this," he replied. Then he added, "You let me worry about North. And yes, why not a little extra fun?"

"Do you have any idea what this will look like to Mike and everyone else at work?"

"That loser? I don't give a shit what he thinks."

"I do," I snapped. "Jesus, if he finds out we slept together, he'll think I did it to get this deal to go through."

He frowned. "Why do you let him bother you?"

"Because he's aiming for the same corner office I am and there's only room for one of us."

He shook his head ever so slightly, as if I'd somehow disappointed him with my answer. I was angry at him, but I felt that... lack of understanding deep inside.

"Look, North will sign because you put one hell of a contract together. You think she'd let anyone think shit like that?"

I held up my hand. God, why didn't he understand? "It's easy for you because you're a freaking lumberjack and a billionaire."

His eyes narrowed and he went still, which was odd because he was calm to begin with. "Money doesn't solve every problem, half pint."

I'd touched a nerve and I didn't know enough about him to know what it was. So I shifted it back to me. "Everyone lowers their morals to get that corner office, but I refuse to do so. I work my ass off and now a few hours naked yesterday with you could destroy me. The truth doesn't matter. It happened. I *did* sleep with the client. Worse, I slept with the patent holder himself."

"I'm sure Mike's had sex before."

I didn't want to picture that.

"Not with a client because I'm pretty sure he'd

flaunt that." I sighed. "I did the *one* thing he couldn't accomplish."

"Dinner!"

North's call was muffled, but we heard it. So did the dog because he popped up and stood at the closed door, tail wagging, waiting for West to open it.

"Finish up, half pint." He pointed to my cell on the desk. "Your client's calling you to eat."

I took a breath, trying to get the importance of my goal across to him. "I'm getting the promotion, West. I am. I've worked too hard to lose it now because of hot sex with a player."

A slow smile spread across his face.

"What?" I asked.

"Hot sex, huh?"

I rolled my eyes and growled.

"Ooh, she has claws. Maybe I should call you kitten instead."

5

EST

AS JED HANDED me a plate loaded with egg casserole, I eyed the two women sitting across from each other. While they looked nothing alike, North and Rory were very similar. They were smart, successful and driven. They worked too much. Or at least Rory sure as shit did. Thankfully, Jed had curbed North's ways. She'd practically burned herself out and I lived down the road and let it happen. For years.

That was on me for not seeing what she'd been doing. Burying herself in the job as a way to survive with Macon. To satisfy him in some long term deal me and my brothers never even knew about. We'd blindly thought she lived for that shit, when in fact, she'd lived like she had to protect us. She'd bargained with the asshole to work at the family's company so that her three younger brothers could have the lives they wanted. South was a sculptor. East was a math professor. I'd gone off to MIT for two years, but my real desire had been to ranch. To run the family land, but because of Macon, I'd purchased a property nearby and worked it instead.

We'd done what we wanted at a hefty price to North. One she'd willingly paid. Yeah, that was on me. South and East too.

Macon was dead. Out of our lives for good.

North had Jed who loved her and protected her fiercely. Ensured she had a life where she was fulfilled —finally—as CEO now but also happy.

Yeah, fucking happy.

These days, she smiled.

She still wore those ridiculous power suits but away from the office, she was just North in sweats and her hair in a sloppy ponytail.

Like right now.

Laughing at something Jed told her as she nibbled a piece of bacon. Not thinking about work.

Then there was Rory.

Total workaholic. Control freak. Gorgeous. Smart. Sexy. Wound tighter than any person I'd ever met. Except when I had her beneath me and my cock buried deep inside her.

I wanted to be pissed at North for bringing her here because having her sitting beside me, eating my favorite casserole, was messing with me.

I had no idea why the hell I was into her. She was a pain in my ass. Irrationally angry and it seemed all that wildness was focused my way. She had fucking claws and seemed to want to sink them into me. That made my dick hard which made me either a masochist or an idiot.

Because instead of leaving the office and driving to my ranch, I'd come here. Rory Sullivan was *everything* I wasn't looking for. Except for the fact that she was highly intelligent and could hold her own with me. Hell, she even stood up to me. Not many did because of my size or the fact that I was a Wainright. People thought having a shit ton of money made me different. Made me better or something.

It had been a pain in my ass since birth. Sure, it didn't hurt to know I wasn't going to go cold or hungry, but it didn't ensure happiness or love. Our mother died when I was two. I didn't even remember her. I did remember Macon, who we'd assumed was our father until last summer after he'd had a heart attack and died in bed with his male lover.

Yeah, that had been a surprise.

What was more of one was that North, East and I weren't his. Only South.

We had no idea who our sperm donor was.

Still, we'd been stuck with Macon and his hatred. All four of us kids would have given every penny away for a living mother and a loving father.

Everyone had to play the cards that were dealt. With Macon gone, I was closer with my brothers and sister now. Which made me see North was up to something.

I had no doubt I'd played right into whatever game she had going because here I was. Probably just as she'd expected.

There was no way she knew I'd given Rory a very special, and naked, welcome to Montana. I hadn't told her because *that* was never going to happen. Rory had made it very clear that being with me—West Wainright, not Weston the Ranch Hand—was a big mistake.

Maybe mine was being here. I should just take my plate and head home, forget Rory Sullivan and her sexy moans and clenching pussy. That would be the smart thing because she'd made it crystal clear she was moving into a corner office in a different area code. All because of this deal. My patents. In a way, because of *me*. Nothing was going to stop her from that. If that was her dream, then she should go for it, even if working eighty hours a week killed her to get there. I just wasn't going to be her man while she did it. Been there, done that with Carrie.

I was happy. Content.

Then why the fuck was I here?

Because my dick was in charge at the moment. Because I wanted to see her again. I wanted to get her to bend to my will. To get her on her knees. To get inside her and watch her give over. It had been powerful and stunning to witness.

I wanted to be with her.

"Have you ever been to Montana before?" Jed asked Rory as he scooped casserole onto his own plate now that he'd served everyone else.

She had her fork halfway to her mouth when she shook her head.

"What do you think?" he added.

A smile spread. "It's beautiful. Different than New York."

North laughed. "Definitely. I missed it here when I was in Boston."

"Harvard, right?" Rory asked.

"Yes." North tipped her head my way. "He was at MIT and couldn't hack it."

I rolled my eyes.

Rory looked to me as she chewed. I had no idea what she was thinking.

"Two years was enough for me," I explained.

I wasn't sharing how I'd been burned by Carrie and her greed and need to be with a Wainright. A degree was obviously the end goal of going to college, but I'd gone to escape Macon first and foremost. But once I got there and had the Carrie mind fuck, I'd realized I didn't give a shit if I got one. I'd been bored with my classes and wanted to be back in Montana. MIT on my resume wasn't required if I ranched.

"You went to Columbia," North said, looking to Rory.

"You did your research, too," she replied, tucking her sleek hair behind her ear. "But yes. Undergrad and law school."

"You're a city girl."

"Born and raised." And clearly proud of it.

"You work in your family's firm. You must be close."

North's words had Rory tense. It was subtle, but I saw it. Rory took the napkin from her lap and dabbed her lips as if to take a moment. "My father's firm. He's a founding partner. It's not really a family affair. Just me following his footsteps and only an associate. My older brother is a doctor. Neurosurgeon."

An impressive family.

"But you're making partner," I added, because there was no way I could forget that since she'd shoved it down my throat more than once. I cut off a section of casserole with my fork and shoved *that* in my mouth.

She nodded. "Yes."

Based on the way North's eyebrows went up at Rory's answer, Rory hadn't told North she was getting that position. I assumed it was because Rory would get it when closing the deal with North. I respected Rory for that discretion, ensuring that the contract was signed solely because of solid negotiations and nothing else.

"Impressive," North answered. "Your parents should be proud."

It wasn't something North had never gotten from Macon. Family pride.

Rory shrugged. "My mother thinks I should quit and join her on the luncheon and spa circuit. Run charities while the boys make the deals."

If her dad was a founding partner of a New York City law firm, one that was prestigious enough to be on retainer for the engineering corporation after my patents, then the Sullivans had money. Especially based on the lifestyle her mom seemed to have. Rory's clothes were professional, but not expensive. I wasn't a fashion expert, but I could spot excess across forty acres. She'd flown commercial to get to Montana. She hadn't taken a private jet and her hotel room hadn't been a suite.

She was high maintenance, but not... difficult. She worked hard. Too fucking hard for a debutante.

North stabbed a piece of melon. "I do like my shoes," she replied diplomatically.

That made Rory laugh. "I do too."

"I love the black patent ones you're wearing."

So did I. *Fuck, so did I.*

"The perks of living in New York. Shoe stores."

North sighed, as if she was missing out. "I've organized for your bag from the hotel to be delivered and will arrive sometime soon, although I doubt you've got any cowgirl boots packed to wear."

Rory smiled. "No. Definitely not."

"West will take you to the feed and seed in town for a pair."

I arched a brow and eyed North as Rory raised a hand. "That's okay."

"You're here for the weekend," North countered, confirming that Rory wasn't getting out of here before Monday. "Those gorgeous heels can't get all muddy."

"I'll take you," I said, and Rory's head whipped my way. A pretty flush crept up her cheeks and I couldn't help but smile at her dirty mind. I'd take her to get some boots, then see her wearing them... and nothing else as *I took her.*

"As for this weekend," Rory began, pushing a piece of casserole around on her plate and steering the conversation away from subtle innuendo.

North glanced at Jed, then back to Rory. "I'll sign the contract."

"You... but—"

"I'll sign it for you. Not Mansplaining Mike."

That made Rory laugh, and fuck, she was pretty.

"There will be no question when you go back on Monday that you're the one who closed the deal. You did all the work." When Rory was about to say more, North held up her hand to stop her. "Don't even think of saying that Mike knows his ass from his elbow."

Rory shook her head and clearly tried to hide a smile. "Never."

"Good. Then finish up. It's Friday night. I feel like shooting some things."

North grabbed for another piece of bacon.

I glanced at Rory. She was staring at North, a little

shell shocked. Her thoughts were as obvious as a billboard in Times Square. *Shooting?* There weren't any dance clubs or symphonies out here so we made our own kind of fun.

Reaching out, I patted her arm. "Don't worry. I'll show you how to shoot." And get my hands on her again when I did so. Fuck yeah, this was going to be fun.

6

ORY

NORTH MUST FIGURE she was helping, but really, it was only making the situation worse. Keeping me here in Montana, in her mind, made it very clear that I was the one she was working with to finalize the contract. I could return to New York confident that I'd closed the deal. Not Mike.

I appreciated her *girls have to stick together* mindset, except everyone at work would question it. Especially Mike. My father already had, based on the phone call a little earlier. They'd all wonder why she had me stay. No one in New York offered up the kind of hospitality where they took a client home with them for the weekend. The concept was completely foreign. It didn't happen. Ever.

Because of that, they'd skip right past the possibility of it being *nice* to think deeper. I was hogging the client for myself. I had some kind of agenda. If it were anywhere but Montana, some would think I was trying for another job. Networking myself into a position at the company.

Except this was *Montana* and everyone knew I had my focus squarely on becoming partner.

I was even wondering... why was I here? North had said she'd sign. So why didn't she just do so? Why was *West* even here? Yes, this house was his house as much as his sister's, but he lived on his own property. The egg casserole was good, but not *that* good. He sure as hell didn't look—or feel—like he couldn't feed himself and had to get his meals made by the family chef.

Besides all that were my feelings toward him. My anger and frustration at being used still lingered. I'd wanted sex. I'd propositioned him. I couldn't blame him for saying yes. It had been good. *Really* good and the man was distracting as hell. It'd been hard at the meeting to focus with his super-sized presence at the end of the table. He hadn't said a word once we'd gotten started, but I'd known he was there.

My ovaries hadn't stopped reminding me of how gorgeous and talented he was.

Even eating dinner with him, innocently enough. And then now. He was a distraction I didn't want. I *couldn't* have. Because the first time had been a mistake and was going to be an issue, but I still wanted him. No woman in her right mind wouldn't want more of what we'd done in my hotel room. Or whatever else he might want to do to me. *With* me.

My panties were ruined. Again.

I had so much work to do and yet I wouldn't be able to focus with him nearby. Not now, knowing what it was like between us. The chemistry was insane. The continued desire for him was powerful. And wrong.

Work! I couldn't be sidetracked.

Except I was standing out on the lawn of a family of billionaires in my bare feet and ear plugs dangling around my neck. Work was *not* going to happen. Jed stood by the skeet trap as North readied her shotgun. West was beside me, showing me how to load bullets into the weapon.

Talk about mansplaining.

"It's going to be loud and there's some kick, so make sure the butt of the gun is pressed firmly against your shoulder."

What West didn't know was I knew how to shoot.

A woman needed to know how to protect herself even outside of the Wild Wild West. Looking around, I took in the gorgeous, billion-dollar view. There wasn't anyone for miles. No one could sneak up and try to mug me or anything worse. Out here, I was more afraid of wild animals than wild humans. But just because I didn't own a gun didn't mean I didn't know how to use one and use it well. My freshman roommate's family owned a gun range on Long Island and her overprotective father had ensured I learn how to shoot as well, single women in the city and all that.

Except we were doing this for *fun,* not protection. No range. No need for a lane reservation or a gun license or whatever. This was very private land and North wanted to shoot some shit. Not my typical Friday night, but when in Montana and all that.

I hadn't told any of them that I knew what I was doing, so it wasn't West's fault he was going over something I already had down. He was trying to be helpful, his directions clear and succinct. I just nodded and watched because, well, I was going to have my own kind of fun.

I had to admit, it was really pretty here. Crazy pretty. Rolling hills, waving grass, snowcapped mountains. No honking horns. No city stench. No concrete. No parents nearby.

The sun hadn't set yet and the air was warm. Soft. Peaceful. And I had no idea what to do with it.

Except shoot the shit out of stuff.

West stepped close, reached out and I held my breath. I didn't know what he was going to do and I breathed in his crisp scent. Man and woods—which there weren't any around here—and leather. Enticing.

Except he didn't do anything except lift the ear plugs and settle them into place. He leaned down and looked in my eyes, asking if they were comfortable. I nodded and bit my lip, because, fuck, I'd thought he was going to kiss me.

That answered my question about what I wanted from him.

Out of the corner of my eye, I saw Jed pull a rope which launched a clay target. North swung her gun up and shot it to pieces. She grinned as she pointed her weapon to the ground, walked over to Jed and he tugged her into his arms to kiss the top of her head.

I hadn't seen a relationship like theirs before. Ever, maybe. My parents didn't love each other, at least not in any outwardly affectionate way. They had more of a... business arrangement. I'd never seen them hug. Or my dad take a second to stand still long enough to be affectionate. I had to wonder how my brother and I had even been conceived.

Watching the couple, I felt an ache, a longing for something I didn't even know I wanted. I couldn't imagine being that close with a man. Sharing a life. Dreams. Affection.

Then I blinked and focused on West, who still hadn't looked away. His gaze was on my lips.

"Ready?" he asked, standing to his full height.

I could hear him through the ear plugs and I nodded, taking a second to pull myself together. I was having ridiculous visions of West and me... like that.

Yeah, no. He was rough and bossy. A pain in my ass.

The cowboy and the city slicker. That was *never* going to happen.

He led me to stand where North had been and moved in behind me. *Directly* behind me. He handed me the shotgun and then wrapped his arms around me to help me position it properly.

I let him help because... yeah, he felt good. He was warm at my back. He was so much bigger than me without my heels, he could set his chin on top of my head. His thick arms felt protective around me and I felt the thick, hard press of his dick against my back. I wasn't the only one affected.

His words were soft and soothing, although that could have been because I was wearing ear plugs. "Set it here. Good. Put your finger on the trigger. Gently. Good girl."

I preened at that term. *Good girl.* He'd used it before and fuck, it was hot. Reassuring. The mild praise made me shiver. Why did two words out of his mouth make me feel confident and special at the same time?

"This too much?" he asked. "I can set up some cans for you to shoot instead."

I cleared my throat because he was being remarkably thoughtful. No one ever took the time to ask what I wanted. If I was okay. Happy. I shook my head which bumped against his chest. "I'm good."

"Okay, I'll stay right here with you as you shoot. Don't want you flying back."

I took a deep breath, let it out. Why was he affecting me now? Why did I feel like I wanted to cry? Not because he hurt my feelings. No, it was because he made me *feel.* To know a guy could actually be just... nice.

And then I pulled up my big girl panties because he was also the guy who annoyed the shit out of me. He probably was thoughtful to all the women who came and shot skeet with his family.

"Ready?"

I nodded. Jed pulled the rope and I followed the

arc of the target with the barrel of the gun and fired. The clay exploded. It was loud and there was a kick, just as West had said, but I'd expected it. I aimed the weapon down as West moved around to stand in front of me.

He smiled at me, eyes filled with wonder.

Jed and North were laughing, although I couldn't see them around West's super-sized body.

"You can shoot," he said.

"Yes." I felt exhilarated. And smug.

"Again."

He went and grabbed North's gun from her and traded it with mine. I popped it open, checked the bullets, then clicked it shut with an ease of familiarity. West settled beside me this time, hands on his hips. I looked to Jed and said, "Pull."

I followed the target once again. Fired. The pieces rained down over the lawn.

West came over, took the gun from me. Leaned down and whispered in my ear. "Holy shit, kitten. That's fucking hot."

He took my hand and tugged me along as he handed Jed the gun.

"We're out of here."

Jed arched a brow but said nothing. North had her

fingers over her lips as if trying not to laugh as she looked to her brother.

"Out of here?" I parroted.

West looked down at me with a heat and intensity that had me taking a small step back. His hand holding mine kept me from going any further. "Your choice, kitten. Walk or I carry."

Walk or carry?

I set my free hand on my hip. "Listen here, you bossy oaf, I can't—"

"Carry it is."

He bent at the waist and tossed me over his shoulder.

"West!" I cried as he stalked off, not toward the house, but around it.

"What about her things?" North called. She wasn't trying to rescue me. What the hell?

"Yeah, what about my things?" I asked, staring at his perfect ass as it flexed with each broad step he took.

"You won't need 'em."

 EST

"THIS IS KIDNAPPING."

I slowed my truck and pulled over on the side of the dirt road between the big house and mine. "Hop on out, kitten."

She looked out the window, her spine straight as a fence post. The sun had set and the colors across the prairie were changing. It was my favorite time of day in the summer, this lingering twilight.

"Are you serious?" she sputtered. "I have no idea where we are and I have no shoes."

No, I wasn't fucking serious. Like I would leave her, or any woman, on the side of the road. But she'd been sitting, arms crossed and fuming, since I carried her off.

Why was I putting myself through this? I had no fucking idea. No. I did. My dick was running my life right now and my dick wanted Rory and while this banter was fun and all, it was wasted time where we could be naked instead. With my dick in her mouth.

That would quiet her, although I wasn't sure if she might bite it off.

"Why are you doing this? Is it because I can shoot?"

"Yes," I replied, shifting in my seat.

For some reason, her being a crack shot was hot as fuck. The fact that she'd kept it a secret and made me feel like an ass for practically treating her like a five-year-old with a cap gun only made my dick-to-zipper situation even worse.

The woman had balls. Big fucking balls.

The sooner I got her in my bed and begging, the better. So I started driving again. I'd turn the truck around and drop her off with North if she was truly upset. Except I'd been around her enough now to recognize her attitude was most likely a self-defense mechanism. That I was pushing her in ways she couldn't control. Hell, as she said, she was barefoot and was ten miles from the nearest town.

"If I were a man, you wouldn't be pissed."

"If I were a man, I wouldn't have tossed you over my shoulder to take you home with me so we can fuck whatever this is out of our system."

Her mouth hung open.

"Yeah, kitten. I'm not mad. I'm fucking horny. You keep surprising me."

"You're such a player," she grumbled, crossing her arms.

"You keep saying that. How have I played you?" he asked. "You're the one who propositioned me. I had no idea you were tackling my patents. I had no idea my sister would fly you back to her ranch for the weekend. All I'm doing is giving us what we both want."

"I don't have time to fuck."

She flung her hands in the air. Did she even hear what she was saying? If anyone needed to fuck, it was someone who said they didn't have time for it.

"I have work to do."

I rolled my eyes. "No one who's doing it right ever says they don't have time to fuck. Things were pretty fucking hot in your hotel room, but now I have to apply myself more."

"We're going to... to what? Go to your place and have sex all weekend?"

I couldn't help the slow smile that spread across my face. "I knew you were smart."

"I have work to do, West."

"Jesus, enough with the work, work, work. No, you don't."

"Yes, I do."

I sighed, squeezed the steering wheel. We could go back and forth all night. "Fine. You have work, but you're not doing it this weekend."

Her gaze narrowed and she glared. "Don't you have cows to milk or hay to bale or something?"

I ignored the question. "Kitten. That fucker Mike and the other guys are on a plane right now. They're not working." I glanced at the clock on the dash. "Your daddy sure as shit isn't working at eleven on a Friday night."

The time difference put the guy I was liking less and less in his jammies by now. Why didn't he get his daughter to work less and have a life?

"I don't even have my phone," she countered.

"To do what, play Solitaire?"

She huffed. "I have projects. Clients."

"Again, Friday night."

"I *need* to be connected. How long do you plan on keeping me?"

That was a loaded question and one I didn't want to think about too hard, because I might not like the answer.

"Until you wind the shit down."

"Impossible," she countered.

I grinned as I turned down my drive. "Challenge accepted, kitten."

"You and your tiny dick can fuck yourself."

I looked her over, winked. "You are very familiar with my dick and know it's far from tiny. And I do the fucking around here."

I pulled up in front of the house and shifted to face Rory, setting my forearm on the steering wheel. "What's so wrong about taking time for yourself?" I asked, my voice quieter. "I'm not asking you to muck stalls. I'm going to fuck you until you forget your name. Don't lie and say you didn't enjoy it at the hotel when I crammed you full of my dick and made you scream. I'd swear you even squirted that second time."

Her face turned even redder and her eyes narrowed. If they could shoot lasers, I'd be Swiss cheese. She pursed her lips. "I told you, to make partner—"

"Yeah, you told me." Like a broken record. "Try

again. You sleep, don't you?"

She only glared some more.

"So take time for yourself while you're conscious... and riding my dick."

"West," she said, drawing out my name.

"North told you she'd sign the contract," I tossed out.

Rory was like a dog with a bone and while I knew once she'd had a few orgasms and was more pliant than a piece of plywood, she'd see how work could wait. But now? I wasn't going to force a woman into my bed. She just needed to be able to justify a few fucking seconds of free time in that busy mind of hers. If she was to have that corner office after this deal like she said, she'd have already earned it. A weekend without her cell connected to her hand wasn't going to prevent it from happening.

"Everyone thinks you're with the client," I added. "Which you are. You can bill the shit out of this. I'm sure you're not the first lawyer to bill a client for time in the sack."

"That's all this is." She waved her hand around.

I frowned, not getting her.

"I don't prostitute myself for work. I mean, all this is is time in the sack," she clarified. "I need to work, but if you're going to hold me prisoner—"

"I'll tie you to my bed so you aren't called a liar."

I shifted in my seat at the thought. So did she.

"You don't want this, kitten, I'll take you back to the big house. Spend the weekend with North and Jed. I promise you though, she won't let you work either. Why do you think she brought you out here?"

She frowned.

"She sees herself when she looks at you, I'm guessing." I reached out, stroked her cheek with my knuckles. So fucking soft.

"If they find out we had sex—"

"Then a few more times isn't going to change anything," I finished. "If they're going to fuck you over at your office when you get back, you might as well get a few more orgasms out of it."

"West," she began.

"Just the weekend in my bed. Don't worry, you'll get your signed contract and a ride to the airport. I'm not keeping you."

I wasn't. She had her life and I had mine. But we could have fun, for now.

———

RORY

. . .

WEST HAD TOSSED me over his shoulder and carried me off. Holy shit, *that* had been hot. Not that I would ever tell him. Because I didn't want him to think I liked him having that kind of power over me. My vagina was all for it though. In fact, as he led me onto the front porch, my hand in his big one, I realized he was going to learn the truth of that fact when he discovered how wet my panties were.

I could say all kinds of things to make him think I hated him and his dick, but my pussy didn't lie.

Traitor.

Besides it being hot, it was annoying that he'd dragged me off. I hadn't said goodbye to North or Jed. He might as well have dragged me away by the hair, club in hand, the Neanderthal.

I didn't have my laptop. Or phone. Or shoes. Or hair conditioner. Or noise machine for sleeping. He didn't understand that I had things to do. Besides *doing* him.

"I can hear you mentally plotting a coup from here, kitten."

I huffed. "This whole caveman routine work on other women? Because it's not—"

"I don't bring women here," he admitted, cutting me off.

My mouth hung open with my unfinished

sentence. And surprise.

"Why not? I mean, I'm here."

He gave me a look that I couldn't translate.

"Yeah, well... I wasn't fucking you in my old bedroom at the big house. I walked out of there when I headed to MIT and haven't spent a night there since. Not going to start now. Especially when what I have planned for you involves you screaming my name."

"That could also mean you plan to murder me."

He gave me a look, the corner of his mouth tipping up. "I don't hurt women. Ever."

I swallowed, nodded. I'd insulted him and that hadn't been my intention.

"Look. I took away your laptop and your phone. I carried you off. It's all my fault. Not yours."

Oh, hell no. "You didn't take them away. That implies you have them and aren't giving them back. You *left* them behind. I don't have a choice."

He tipped his head to the side in that ridiculously chill way of his. "I'm curious how that smart brain of yours thinks you ever had a choice when you were with me. I'll keep you safe, kitten. From everything." He leaned in. "Other than allowing me to touch your gorgeous body, you aren't the one in charge."

"I hate you," I muttered. I'd never known anyone who'd pretty much vowed to protect me. *From every-*

thing. And that was part of the reason I said that. I was starting to like him and that was ridiculous.

"If that helps you justify what we're going to do, I'm good with that."

I sputtered, but he turned away and went to the front door. He didn't unlock it, just pushed it open. I had to wonder if he thought he could fight off an intruder on his own—which was certainly possible—or if we were so far out in the middle of nowhere nothing ever happened.

The house reminded me of the one in the American Gothic painting, although I didn't envision West in overalls with a pitchfork. This was my first farmhouse because Billionaire Ranch was far from modest. In comparison, West's house was... normal. White siding. A rocking chair on the wraparound porch. I expected a golden retriever to greet us, tail wagging. The scent of fresh baked cookies coming from the kitchen.

I didn't have time to do more than glance at the entry with the simple rug and side table before the door slammed behind us, I was pressed against it and his mouth was on mine.

His hands reached around and cupped my ass as his knee settled between mine. With our height differences, I was pretty much dirty dancing his thigh. The hem of my dress rode up and I gripped his biceps as best I could, but they were like rock beneath my fingers.

"You don't have to overthink this, over what you should be doing. I've taken the decision away. You can't do anything but relax. Have fun. Feel good."

"It's not that simple," I breathed, leaning up so I could kiss him.

"Yeah, it fucking is," he countered, then put his mouth back on mine. His hands were on my hips, holding me still. "Now stop talking or I've got something to stick in that mouth."

I launched myself at him—surprising both of us—and kissed the hell out of him.

"Well, kitten," he murmured when he eventually started to kiss along my jaw. "If the thought of sucking my dick gets you running hot then—"

Hot? I was burning. Needy. I'd never been like this with anyone before. I didn't understand it. "Stop talking or I've got a pussy that needs licking."

He growled and nipped my ear lobe.

"I'm not taking you like this again," he said, rolling his hips and I couldn't miss the impressive bulge in his jeans. "Fuck, woman, I can't get past the door with you but I needed a taste, my hands on you." He stepped back and pointed to the stairwell. "I have to lock up.

Upstairs. I want you on my bed, naked, legs spread by the time I get up there."

I wasn't sure why he was locking up *now,* but I was so turned on by what he'd just told me to do. I could argue, but all it would do was make it longer before he got inside me. Doing it out of spite only delayed my own pleasure.

He was right. It was his fault that I was here. I couldn't work. Couldn't check voicemail or even read the news. All I had to do was obey and I'd be satisfied.

Standing there, he crossed arms over his barrel chest. Waiting patiently, although the thick bulge at the front of his jeans was proof of how turned on he was.

I spun on my bare feet and went toward the stairs, but West reached out and snagged my wrist. He pulled me back and gave me a kiss, this one sweet and gentle. For a guy so big and rough, this felt almost... tender. "Good girl."

Fuck. I was in trouble here.

Those words were going to be my undoing. My compliance made him happy. I didn't have to prove myself. Throw hours at a project. Kill myself to be better than anyone else to receive some form of praise.

No. West just wanted me to be... me. And that was something I didn't understand at all.

8

 EST

I GAVE her a minute upstairs as I caught my breath. My dick was throbbing to get inside her and my mouth watered to lick her pussy. I wanted to see what Rory would do, if she'd listen or if she'd climb out the bedroom window and escape. Except there was nowhere for her to go. Not that I'd hold her here. Yes, technically I'd kidnapped her, but if she were truly losing her shit, not just spitting mad, I'd take her back to North. Hell, I'd drive her to the airport myself.

But she didn't like being out of control and with only the clothes on her body, she was at my mercy.

Yet she'd walked up the steps willingly and was... shit, I had to shift my dick in my pants thinking about it, most likely stripping bare. No woman would do that if she wasn't running hot, even if every word out of her mouth told me otherwise.

By taking her, I'd given her permission to let go. So while she might say she hated me, she *loved* my dick. And I was going to give it to her.

When I entered my bedroom, I paused. "Fuck," I breathed.

Her dress was on the floor along with her lacy bra and panties. She was in the center of my bed, leaning back on her elbows in a pose that looked planned. Seductive. It was the look in her eyes, the hint of nerves that had me thinking she didn't realize just how fucking gorgeous she was. That giving her even a bit of time alone had her losing her nerve.

I wasn't going to let that happen.

Placing my knee on the bed, I crawled up and over her, settling my hands on either side of her body. Our mouths were close and I looked into her green eyes.

"Such a good girl listening," I murmured. "Widen those pretty thighs for me. I want to see how wet my pussy is."

Yeah, it was mine. At least while I had her in my bed.

The thought of another guy seeing her like this made me growl.

She slid her feet across the bed, bending her knees even more.

I sat back on my heels and looked her over. Flushed cheeks. Upturned, full breasts. Nipples pink and tight. Soft curves. And... fuck...

Some were ass men. Some boob men. Me? I was all about the pussy and hers so fucking pretty. Neatly trimmed, her inner folds were large enough to peek out, swollen and glistening. I didn't need a fucking map to find her clit. It was right there at the top, a hard little pearl.

"*My* pussy?" she sassed as she tried to close her legs.

I flicked my gaze up to hers, keeping her spread wide with my palms on her silky thighs. "You mentioned a pussy that needed licking? *My* tongue, *my* pussy."

She sucked in a breath as I settled between her spread legs because if she wanted to say my dick was hers right before she put her mouth on it, I wouldn't care. I cupped the backs of her knees and lifted one, then the other over my shoulders. She flopped onto her back when I licked her from bottom to top, collecting all that sticky sweetness that was just for me.

A hand went over her eyes as she rolled her hips.

"Make all the noise you want, kitten. We're not doing anything else until you come all over my face. So shut that shit down, let go and give it to me."

My dick was pressed into the mattress and it didn't like the idea of holding back. It wanted inside of her, sliding deep like my finger was. She was dripping, hot and clenching. Tight and perfect. But it was my fucking goal in life right now to get that smart brain of hers to go quiet.

I watched her to see what she liked. A flick on the left side of her clit instead of a swirl. A shallow curl with my finger instead of deep thrust. Her thighs quivered. Her heels pressed. Her gasps and cries spurred me on. I could stay here for hours, teasing her. Getting her to beg.

But my dick couldn't handle it. Not this time.

I sat back again, her ankles now hooked over my shoulders.

"No! What is *wrong* with you?" she shouted, fingers clenching my blanket.

I wiped my mouth with the back of my hand, then worked open my pants, pushing them down enough so I could pull myself out. "My dick's hard. Needs in you."

I turned and flopped down onto the bed beside her, making her rise up as if on a trampoline.

"Come sit on my face, kitten."

She shifted onto her side and stared at my dick, which was dripping pre-cum and so hard it was brushing my navel. I crooked a finger.

"Straddle me."

I helped her upright and she swung a leg over my chest. I was so broad and she was so small, her knees didn't rest on the bed. But her pussy was nestled on my chest making it nice and wet.

"Turn around."

She frowned down at me, her hair a curtain that tickled my chest.

Setting my hands on her hips, I lifted her. She gasped and caught on that I was spinning her around.

"Suck, kitten. I promise you'll get all the cream."

I pulled her back so her pussy was right over my face. "So will I."

———

RORY

. . .

OH. My. God.

West's mouth was so talented and his dick... he could be in porn. Long and thick and actually good looking. It was hot against my palm as I gripped it and my mouth watered to taste that pearl of fluid beading at the top.

He growled against my pussy as I took the flared crown into my mouth. We'd been too busy straight-up fucking in the hotel room for me to do this. There was no way I was taking all of him. He was just too big and I'd never taken someone to the back of my throat before.

Using my palm, I stroked him as I took him as deep as I could, then pulled back. It was hard to focus when he slid fingers inside me. It felt like two, but maybe three.

I moaned, popped off and the silky head bopped my chin. "West," I moaned. "I'm close."

"So am I," he replied. "Swallow or let me come on your pretty tits."

His voice was gravelly and rough and he pulsed in my grip.

I wanted to please him, to make him feel as good as he was making me, so I took him as deep as I could, breathing through my nose as I sucked and licked.

The hand that gripped my hip shifted so his thumb pressed against my back entrance. No, not just pressed but pushed in.

Holy fuck! I came instantly, milking his fingers and rolling my hips. Filled in both holes and his mouth sucking on my clit. I moaned and sucked harder, lost.

A deep groan came from his chest and vibrated across my pussy as I felt his dick swell in my mouth followed by the hot pulses of his cum on my tongue. I swallowed, again and again to keep up with the amount of his release.

I pulled off, catching my breath. One last spurt hit my chin, warm and... so dirty.

He maneuvered me again how he wanted, spinning me about once more so he was kissing me. I tasted myself on his lips and I had to wonder if he could taste his seed on my tongue. It smeared across his jaw.

"Ass play sets you off," he said when I lifted my head. He stroked my hair back.

He didn't care that he had his cum on his face or that it mixed with my arousal that coated his five o'clock shadow. Sex wasn't tame or civilized. It was wild and we got sweaty, sticky and dirty.

My cheeks flushed. "I... um. Yeah." I didn't want to admit it, but he knew the truth. Felt it.

With one hand over my back, he tilted and grabbed a condom from his bedside drawer. He pushed me back so I straddled his thighs and handed me the ripped open package.

"Put this on and take me for a ride, kitten," he murmured.

I looked down. He was hard. Really hard. Hard like he hadn't just come in my mouth.

"Again?" I whispered.

My pussy clenched because while I'd come, I felt empty now. I wanted him in me.

"Not a chance we're done. I've got a list, kitten."

A list. I wasn't sure if my body was up for a *list*. I needed vitamins or something to keep up.

I tossed the wrapper aside and rolled the condom down his thick length as he undid the buttons on his shirt. He was barely undressed, but it made it even hotter. Me naked with him half-unwrapped.

"Tomorrow, we'll go horseback riding. Ever been?" he asked.

I shook my head. I had his protected dick in my hand and I wasn't sure why we were talking about horses.

"No."

"It's easy. Climb on, kitten. Riding a horse is just like riding a dick."

The corner of his mouth tipped up and I had to wonder if whenever I did ride a horse that I'd be thinking about this moment.

I pushed up onto my knees, shifted so he was right beneath me and lowered down. I was still wet from the orgasm and he slid in easily. I set my hands on his chest to slow the pace of his penetration because... big.

"Fuck," he murmured, his hands going to my hips and squeezing.

I remained still once I was fully seated.

"Ride, kitten. Up and down. Nice and slow to start. That's it." He coached me as I began to move. "Find what feels good. Yeah, like that? Shit, you feel incredible." His hands began to lift and lower me, faster and harder. My breasts bounced but I didn't care. It felt so good.

"Touch yourself."

I did as he said, reaching between us and rubbing my fingers over my hard clit. I was still worked up so it didn't take long to come. My head tipped back and my eyes fell closed as I came, milking and riding West through the most intense pleasure yet.

He came with me, thrusting deep and holding me down. I slumped on him and rested across his bare, sweaty chest. My eyes were closed and I couldn't help the smile.

"Good girl," he whispered, stroking my hair. That was the last thing I remember before I fell asleep.

9

ORY

"Let's go, kitten. Wastin' daylight."

West's voice woke me, but it was his smack on my ass that had me jumping up.

I sat in his bed, bleary eyed, pushing my hair back. "What time is it?" I asked, looking around for a clock. The sun was shining and West stood before me in his usual uniform of jeans, t-shirt and work boots. His hat was in his hand.

"Nine."

"Nine?" I practically screeched, looking around for my clothes. "I haven't slept that late since college."

"I'd like to say I wore you out, that you needed some sleep." He winked.

I looked around, the sheets tangled around me, the blanket on the floor. I was sure I looked like I'd been well fucked. Because I had.

"Get dressed and we'll get the day started."

"In what?" I asked.

"I had clothes delivered." He went to a dresser and picked up a neat pile off the top. "I had to guess your sizes a bit, but they should work."

He handed them to me. Jeans, plaid blouse with... were those snaps? Also in the pile was a white camisole, socks, panties and a bra.

"You had clothes delivered. Here. Before nine on a Saturday morning?"

He grinned. "The perks of being a Wainright." His gaze raked over me. I held the white sheet over my breasts even though he'd seen—and touched—all of me. "Meet me downstairs, otherwise I'll stay here and fuck you some more."

He turned on his booted heel and left.

Thirty minutes later, I'd showered and tamed my damp hair into a knot since I didn't have a tie. I'd brushed my teeth with the packaged toothbrush on the vanity and dressed in the provided clothing.

West was pouring coffee at the counter when I

came down the back steps. He took in my *very* western outfit. "Montana looks good on you."

I hadn't worn knee high socks since elementary school and the shirt really was fastened by snaps.

He handed me the steaming mug. "I have one more thing for you," he said, grabbing a box off the kitchen table. He opened the lid and held up a cowgirl boot. They were brown leather with turquoise piping. "Since I kidnapped you without any shoes. Those stilettos you wear do great things for your legs and ass but won't work on the back of a horse."

"Um... thank you."

Next, he went to the stove and collected a plate covered with a cloth. He set it down on the table along with silverware and a napkin. "I saved you breakfast. You worked up an appetite."

This version of West was different. Relaxed, calm. Smiling. He wasn't arguing with me or bossing me around. I also wasn't snapping at him.

Maybe it was all the orgasms.

"I'm guessing I'm not getting my phone back."

"No, ma'am. It's still at North's with the rest of your things. All I want you tempted by this weekend is me."

He tugged off the cloth, leaned against the counter, arms crossed.

There was no reason for me to snap at him. He was

being thoughtful and serving me food. Maybe too much based on how the plate was loaded with scrambled eggs, hash browns and sausage patties.

I dropped into the chair and dug in.

"Eat up. You're going to need it."

I speared some eggs onto my fork. "If we're going to have more sex, I didn't have to get dressed."

He laughed. "You're efficient, I'll give you that. The sight of you naked and riding a horse would probably make me come in my pants. I'm thinking you'd be more comfortable in jeans, my little Godiva."

I took a sip of my coffee, suddenly a little panicked.

He wasn't just a sex magician with a powerful dick wand, but he was rugged and well read. I tried really, *really* hard to hate the guy. Except for the fact he wasn't giving back my phone, I *liked* him.

————

WEST

She'd ridden me. And a horse.

Seen my land. What I did. Hell, who I was.

I'd shown her how to take off a saddle and brush down a horse, although I couldn't get her to feed her mare any treats. Every time she held out a cube of sugar in her flat palm, she chickened out when those big teeth appeared. Turned out, there was something this ballsy woman was afraid of.

"Those patents your client just purchased?" I asked, leading her down the center hallway of the stables.

"Yes?" she asked. When her nose started to get a little pink from the summer sun, I'd found a baseball cap and settled it on her head. She looked young and carefree, her hair wild and long down her back. No makeup. And the casual clothes... she looked amazing in them. I'd called Mrs. Sanchez, North's housekeeper, first thing. She'd found Rory's sizes from her clothes in her suitcase, then collected some items at the feed and seed. My request wasn't unusual. The woman had been with the main house for as long as I could remember. The only difference was that I'd never asked her to help me dress one of my houseguests before. Because I'd never had one.

I pushed open the door to my work room. "This is where I tinker."

Reaching in, I flipped on the light switch, but let her enter first. It used to be a storage room for tack and other supplies, but I'd taken it over and put tables around three of the walls. Shelves held all the tools and supplies I needed. While South was the true welder, I had a little tank in the corner and things I needed to build my latest creations.

As Rory walked around the space, running her hands over the random bits of metal and notebooks, I thought about how she saw this room. The place where I spent a bulk of my time. Where I let my mind work, let it go free. I could explore, try, fail. All of it happened within these four walls. It was a mess, but I knew where everything was. This room was me.

Why I was sharing it with her, I had no idea.

She spun and faced me.

"What are you working on now?" she asked.

I pointed to the half-built valve. She turned and picked it up, studied it.

I took the time to explain what it was, what I intended for it to do. She listened closely and bit her lip as she did so. North would be pissed that I shared this with someone, worried the idea would be stolen and exploited. Macon had tried, after he'd learned how much someone had paid for the rights to my first work. Since then, I'd guarded it close.

Maybe I was being stupid, but I couldn't imagine Rory snagging this random valve concept and building it herself in her New York city apartment. She didn't have a phone with a camera or any other way to steal it. And... I trusted her.

"I'm really impressed," she said, meaning it. The words sank deep, settled in my chest. "This, and the others you've done before. You should be proud of yourself."

I shrugged, set the heavy hunk of metal back on the table, not letting on—like usual—that I was affected. I grabbed my safety goggles and fiddled with them. "Like I said, it's just tinkering."

"Your tinkering closed a multi-million-dollar deal," she countered. "You're selling yourself short."

I shrugged and flicked a glance at her. "I've never cared about that part of it."

"Because you have a shit-ton of money already."

I couldn't argue with that.

"They're wanted. Useful. *Needed*," she continued, getting all fired up. For me. "No one can duplicate your invention without you selling the rights. It's a big deal. Don't you care what they're being used for?"

"That's North's work. I told her with the first one she could do what she wants."

She frowned. "Why? I'd think seeing what they're being used for commercially would be rewarding."

"That's not my style." She didn't understand.

"So you stay in this room, on your land in the

middle of nowhere and are content?" she asked. I *was* content, or I'd thought I had been.

"You stay in your little office in a city full of people yet all alone and are content?" I countered.

Her mouth snapped closed.

"Yeah, kitten, that's what I thought." I ran a hand through my hair. She'd struck a nerve, the fact that I didn't want to show off my work. The more I did, the more flack I used to get. Macon... fuck, he would go to town on my little inventions.

It was North who'd believed in them, who pushed to have their rights sold. Sticking my neck out wasn't worth having it chopped off.

"I do my work my way, you do yours," I said.

She stiffened and I could practically see her hackles go up. The rough edges I always felt were back.

"I would, but you took my phone and laptop."

"Feel free to steal a cow, kitten," I countered.

Her eyes narrowed. My dick hardened.

"Maybe we need to stick to what we do best," she snapped.

"What's that?"

"Sex."

I'd been stupid showing her this room. Exposing myself to her or anyone. So I lashed out. Got her angry, which was the way it seemed we got along best. Having her hate me meant she'd walk right out of my life, no hurt feelings on Monday. Easy.

"Kitten, I think you're right."

I pulled her into me and slammed my lips down on hers. Because the best way to keep from snarling at each other was to keep our mouths occupied.

———

"DON'T animals starve if you don't work?" she asked as I kissed down her spine. Her ass tipped up so I knew she was being sassy and sexy at the same time.

This morning, instead of getting up at dawn and tackling chores, I stayed in bed. After the quick fuck in the stable, we'd returned to my bed and hadn't left except to eat. Now it was a lazy Sunday morning and I'd never shared it with a woman before.

It definitely had its perks.

"I'm a billionaire, kitten," I said, reveling that her skin smelled like me. "I have people. I think you call them executive assistants."

I felt her body shake with laughter beneath my lips.

"Mine don't muck stalls."

"They both deal with shit," I countered. We weren't

arguing. Or fucking, although I had a feeling we'd get to both soon enough.

A smile curled her lips. "If you've got *people,* then why do you work?"

"Why do you?"

"I have something to prove."

"To whom?"

She rolled over and fuck... she was so fucking pretty. Her hair was a mess, her lips swollen. Her nipples hard points and there was a little purple mark on the lower curve of one breast proving I'd been there.

She was relaxed and well fucked and not thinking about torts or briefs or whatever.

"To myself. I've earned that partnership."

I couldn't keep my hands off of her. As she spoke, I stroked my knuckles down her silky skin. "I have no doubt. Then what?"

She didn't answer because I settled beside her and kissed her. My hand kept roaming until I found her core. Wet, swollen and ready for more. I slid a finger into her and her inner walls clenched. Fuck, she was still tight after taking me so many times. Her knees fell open, giving over to me without a fight. Then again, I knew now what she liked, where to curl my finger to get her to gasp and arch her back. I added another, opening her up and readying her for me. She wasn't a virgin, but she was tiny and I was fucking huge. I had to soften her up to be able to take all of me. Every time.

"West," she breathed.

My dick pulsed, ready for another round, ready to take the place of my fingers. My balls drew up when I felt her inner walls milk my finger.

I reached for another condom when my cell rang. I ignored it because whoever it was could fucking wait. I had a pussy to sink into. As I ripped open the foil, it rang again. I wouldn't answer it, especially not after forcing Rory's from her fingers the other day, but I checked the screen.

East.

"Shit," I whispered, then reached for it.

"What?"

"You need to get down here." His voice was flat. Dark. Angry.

He was in Bozeman, almost two hours away.

I shifted to sit on the edge of the bed, feet on the floor. "What happened? Are you okay? Ella?"

Out of the corner of my eye, I saw Rory pull the sheet up over herself, which was a fucking shame. My dick was still hard but going down fast. My fingers were wet and sticky from her and I could pick up her sweet scent.

"We're fine. But there's someone here. Says he's our father."

I popped to my feet. "What the fuck?"

Rory sat up, folded her knees in front of her beneath the sheet and eyed me carefully. I'd been about to sink into her pussy again and now I was pacing bare assed. She was smart enough to know something was up. And it wasn't my dick.

"Yeah."

"You believe him? I mean... why now? Why there? Why not show up at the big house?"

He sighed. "I know nothing. I sent him on his way. For now. I'm meeting him at a diner at noon to stall as I thought you'd want to be here. No, not thought. Get your ass down here."

"What's the point? Give him a cup of coffee and tell him to fuck off."

He was quiet for a minute.

I pulled the cell away from my head thinking the call had been dropped. Not a surprise in this area. "East?"

"I believe him," he said finally.

I ran my hand over my hair. Why the fuck was this happening now? Life was simple. Calm. Macon was dead. North was better. She had Jed. South had Maisy and even East had found his woman and gotten happy. I'd found a woman who wanted to be in my bed... temporarily. It was a perfect arrangement.

Then, with one phone call, it had to go to shit. "Why's that?" I wondered.

"Because you look just like him."

"WHAT'S THE MATTER?" I asked.

"Get dressed," West replied, his voice curt, as he went over to the dresser and pulled out a pair of boxers.

Gone was the man who argued with me as if it were an Olympic sport. The one who'd told me what to do. Who'd given me the best orgasms of my life. Who'd ruined my vagina for all other men.

This version of West was cold. Angry. Stoic. Yet still calm, which now, was a little scary.

I wasn't afraid of him, but of what had been shared on the phone call to make him change so abruptly.

I climbed from the bed, picked up my tossed panties, not eager to put them back on.

"Shit. Sorry. Your bag's on the front porch." He stormed out of the bedroom and bounded down the stairs.

I snagged his t-shirt and threw it over my head, then followed. It was enormous on me, hanging down below my knees. The neck hole was big enough to make it slouch off my shoulder. What had he meant that my bag was here?

Stopping halfway down the steps, I watched as West rolled the familiar piece of luggage inside along with my briefcase.

"It's been here the whole time?" I asked, going the rest of the way and joining him. "I didn't have to wear a shirt with snaps?"

He shook his head. "I doubt there's anything in there that would have worked for riding horses. And no, North had someone drop it off this morning. I saw her text about it at dawn when I usually wake up."

My phone and laptop had been delivered as well. I wanted to yell at him for not telling me I could have been working the past few hours instead of sleeping and having sex, but now didn't seem to be the time.

Especially since I now knew how amazing morning sex and napping was. I was a hypocrite to be angry when I'd enjoyed myself so much.

And what we'd been doing just before the call? I liked that much better than work. God, was he wearing off on me?

"I have to go to Bozeman," he said. "Now."

I blinked. Now? As in… his fingers had just been in me but now he was leaving? My pussy was wet and aching for more, but clearly he wasn't going to return to his task.

"Okay," I replied, because what else was there to say? It wasn't like I was going to be able to stop him. I could sit and work while he was gone.

"You're coming with me."

I was surprised, but I felt a hint of warmth that he wanted me to be with him. "Why?"

"You're heading back to New York."

I blinked again, and felt that warmth seep away. "Now?"

He finally looked up at me on the stairs. Standing there, all sturdy and sexy in his boxers, I felt like I could practically see a storm cloud over his head. I had a feeling the way he'd been with me earlier had been rare, that I'd somehow seen a side of him that didn't often appear.

Now it was gone again.

"You're the one who wanted out of here," he reminded. "Now you want to stay?"

I didn't know how to answer that. We'd just been fooling around. A little bubble isolating us and it had been... amazing. Relaxing, just as he'd pretty much ordered me to do. But then that bubble had popped.

"That was your brother?" I asked, trying to figure out what was so urgent.

"East. Yes."

"He's all right?"

"Yes."

"Then what's—"

"It's a family thing and just because I was finger fucking you five minutes ago doesn't mean you want to know this shit." He sighed, then ran a hand over his head again. "Look, you wanted to leave, kitten. You'll be on the first flight on your way to New York. I'll check with North and make sure the contract is signed. You'll be billing clients again before sundown."

He was saying exactly what I'd wanted Friday night instead of him kidnapping me. But now... two nights with him and I was disappointed. Confused, although I wasn't sure if it was because of how he was reacting or how I was.

He'd gone from playful and aroused to serious and intense standing in his plain boxers.

"But what about—"

He took me in wearing his shirt. My hard nipples were poking against the thin cotton and he knew I had nothing on underneath. I was sore and achy, remembering the feel of those fingers and how he'd taken me hard.

"Us?" He shrugged. "It was fun. You're headed to the corner office. I'm not going to stop you."

He wasn't being harsh, just honest. There wasn't anything between us except sex. Crazy good sex. Oddly enough, I'd even thought we had some kind of connection. That there was more to this than just a fling. That was all I'd wanted at the hotel, propositioning him for a few hours of fun and never see each other again. It was all I'd wanted even after the meeting yesterday when he'd appeared unexpectedly. Even Friday night when he tossed me over his shoulder. All I'd wanted was to go back to New York and put everything that happened behind me. But after yesterday? Last night? This morning? It had been... more.

God, I was being stupid. Of course it was *only* fun. It was the amazing orgasms that had me deluded. I'd never come like I had with West. I never knew it could be like that, that my body was made for such passion.

Hell, I had no idea I even liked it when a guy bossed me around because that was the *last* thing I'd have thoght was my kink.

I'd started this. Propositioned him for a few hours in my hotel room. One and done. Then it had turned into more, but West had clearly stated he wasn't keeping me. He'd told me that as reassurance, not for himself—although maybe for him too—but for me. Now I was having ridiculous thoughts. That we might be something.

Silly. Because he sure as hell wasn't moving to New York. There wasn't any room for his cows or his huge Stetson. I wasn't moving here. Owning a pair of boots didn't make me a cowgirl. I was moving into the corner office.

"I was going to say something else. I just figured that since you were finger fucking me like you said, that maybe you could tell me what's going on."

"Does it matter? Your daddy has you killing yourself for a partnership that probably should have been yours years ago. Stringing you along and playing head games. Sounds very fucking familiar."

"What does that have to do with this?" I asked. "That's not–"

He raised his hand. "Save it, kitten. I know all about asshole fathers. I had one, but not by blood, and it took until he was six feet under to get out from under his shit."

"My father's not an asshole. He's... driven."

He laughed and shook his head. "Whatever helps you sleep at night."

"You're talking about Macon Wainright." I felt like we were having two different conversations at the same time. Except the topic was our fathers. In my research, I'd learned Macon Wainright had died the year before. Heart attack. North had taken over as CEO.

"That's the one."

"You just said he's not really your father."

"That's right."

Holy shit. That wasn't in anything I'd read about the family. Or on the news. He'd just told me a big secret, one I wasn't sure if he realized he'd divulged. I wasn't his lawyer so there was nothing keeping me from blabbing it. To me, the information didn't mean anything. It held no value.

I frowned, considering. "But if... if he's dead, then what did East call you about?"

"A man claiming to be my *real* father showed up on his doorstep." He set his hands on his bare hips since his boxers rode decadently low. It was hard not to take in how amazing his body was. Broad shoulders, barrel chest, chiseled abs. It seemed I had a thing about corded forearms because... yeah. H.O.T. Then there were his sturdy legs with thighs probably bigger around than my waist.

The man was huge. Everywhere. And I knew first-hand. Very biblically.

Wait... had he said *real* father? My eyes widened and I stared. "Wow." I didn't know what to say.

"Yeah, fucking wow. So while I'd love to stay buried in your pussy and forget all about it, this guy's not going away until he gets what he probably came for."

I stayed quiet and waited because I was a little caught up on him staying buried in my pussy. I had a pretty good idea what he was going to say.

"Money."

Yup, I was right. The Sullivan family was rich. Plain and simple. My parents lived on the Upper West Side. I'd gone to private school and had no student loans for college or law school. My grandparents had left me a trust outside of my parents' income and what I earned as an associate. I couldn't live off of that gift forever, but it was a solid nest egg that had helped me purchase my apartment. I'd never wanted for anything... except to be partner.

But West and the rest of the Wainrights? They

were billionaires. So much money they could never spend it even after buying a hundred airplanes. Who would want that many airplanes anyway? Sure, I'd dated a guy in college who had certainly liked the perks of a rich girlfriend, but I'd kicked him to the curb pretty fast.

I had no idea what it was like for West to have people claiming to be long lost relatives just for a piece of their very rich pie. Annoying at best. Cruel, too.

West was so big and brawny it was hard to remember he had feelings and emotions. Pain. Frustration. Anger. Even hurt.

"So it's time for you to go, kitten. I'll get you back to your life because you sure as shit didn't sign up for mine."

"Right. Sure." I knelt in front of my suitcase and started to slide open the zipper to get fresh clothes. Clothes that didn't have snaps or decorative leather detailing. I couldn't help him. I wanted to, although it was crazy to want to be there for him. I didn't know the details other than what he'd just shared, but I wanted to give him a hug. Something.

But I was just a woman he'd fucked. A fling. One he'd forget as soon as he pulled his pickup away from passenger drop off. Except I'd have the feel of him for a little longer. My pussy would be sore for days. I'd spotted a few hickeys in the bathroom mirror that would linger. And the memory of being with him wasn't something I could easily forget.

And that was a problem. Because I shouldn't already be missing a big, burly cowboy.

"I can be ready in a few minutes," I told him.

He nodded, then took the stairs two at a time to get dressed, as if he couldn't wait to get rid of me.

11

EST

"Took you long enough," my twin said as I slid into the booth across from him.

The diner was on the edge of Bozeman just off the highway and visited mostly by truckers and those needing a break from driving. It was clean and well maintained, but the scent of grilled onions and coffee probably permeated the vinyl seats and even the menus.

"I had to drop someone at the airport," I replied.

I hadn't said much on the ride and thankfully Rory wasn't one to chatter to fill in the silence.

She'd used her phone the whole time and I hadn't stopped her, too caught up in my own thoughts to worry about her slipping back into her overworking ways. However, her screen use had been well worth it because instead of parking and walking her in, she'd told me she'd changed her ticket online and I could drop her off. So I had. I'd kissed her and pulled her suitcase from the back, but I'd remained on the curb and watched her walk inside and out of my life.

Yesterday had been pretty fucking amazing, but this *father* shit show didn't give me time to think more about Rory and how much I'd liked her at my ranch. And in my bed. And my fingers in her pussy. And her riding my face.

East eyed me. "Holy shit, you got laid."

A waitress came by to top off East's coffee and to offer me one. I nodded to her and she set a clean mug in front of me and poured the steaming brew to the top. I thanked her and took a sip.

"How the fuck can you tell that?" I asked once the woman was out of earshot.

His blue eyes raked over me, at least what he could see above the edge of the table. I wasn't sure how my plaid button-up gave any clue as to what I'd been up to. "You're relaxed," he said finally.

"Says the man who has to beat the shit out of people to make himself feel better," I countered.

He had the same daddy issues as me, although Macon hadn't intended to break my leg so I wouldn't be able to play football in college like he had for East. My twin was a skilled fighter but had used it to burn off aggression.

"*Had*," he clarified. "I *had* to beat the shit out of people to deal. I do it now only for fun. I relax the old-fashioned way, by fucking my woman."

A lot had changed since he'd met Ella last fall. He rarely fought in competitions now, and only sanctioned ones. With rules.

I narrowed my gaze. "You think I'm relaxed? You called and told me a guy is most likely our father and to hustle to meet up with him. I can't think of anything to make my asshole pucker more than someone else trying to fuck me over."

"Us," East clarified.

"Fine. Us. What's this guy's name?"

He shrugged. "Didn't take the convo that far and I wasn't letting him in my house. Figured the fact that you're his spitting image was enough to have a sit-down with the guy. I don't know where he is. Late to his own meeting." He took a sip of his coffee. "Back to you. You got laid. I assume a cow didn't leave scratches like that on your neck." He pointed at me and his gaze dropped to my right ear.

I raised my hand, felt the skin on my neck sting. Fuck. I hadn't noticed. Hell, I hadn't even looked in the mirror before I got us out of the house.

"You get a cat?"

"Fuck you."

He shook his head, grinned. "No, someone fucked you."

No, I did the fucking. Just like I'd told Rory.

"Who is she?"

"You want to know about my love life *now?*" I glanced around. "Where is he?"

"So it's love, then. 'Bout fucking time." I hated when he ignored me.

I gulped down some coffee so I didn't have to talk.

I thought of Rory. How incredible it had been. How different it was to have a woman in my house. In my bed. I'd never taken a woman there, always either going to a motel or to her place. Even a back storage closet at a bar, but never my ranch.

Rory was different. She wasn't from around here. Didn't know which way was north or south without a busy intersection to guide her. But she sure could shoot. And sass me. And stand up to me. And take my dick like she was made for me.

Fuck.

"Well?"

"Jesus, could you be any more annoying? It's not love. It was a fling. She's gone now. On her way back to New York."

I'd had my fingers inside her one minute, then driving her to the airport the next. I'd been a dick. While she'd tossed me my jeans and slammed the door in my face that first day in her hotel room, this was different. I'd pretty much kidnapped her and then did a one-eighty and pushed her on a fucking plane to get rid of her.

Yeah, that was an asshole move and while I'd acted that way because of this potential long-lost father, it didn't justify my behavior. So yeah, it had been a fling.

His brows went up. "New York? I didn't think you got hard for that type."

I gripped my mug. "We're twins, but that doesn't mean we share what gets us off."

He laughed. "Whatever. You wouldn't be cranky if your piece of tail was still around."

I slid my mug out of the way, leaned my forearms on the worn linoleum, looked him square in the eye. "Don't fucking call her that. I'll have you know that—"

A wink went along with that slick grin. "You handed over your balls to a city slicker."

I wanted to punch him in the face, but it wouldn't be a smart idea in the diner.

He was fucking with me on purpose and I was falling right into his shit. I was pissed he was doing it, but also at my own reaction. If Rory was just a quick fuck I'd never see again, I'd have told him all about how good she was, how she'd kept up with me, let go of all her inhibitions to be a little wildcat—with fucking claws.

I ran my fingers over the scratches again.

Instead, I didn't want even my twin to know about what she and I had done. The fact that I had marks on me meant Rory hadn't been holding back and I'd wear them as a badge of honor. I'd done what I'd set out to do. Get Rory out of her head and on her knees.

I had no idea when she'd become more than a quickie. Maybe seeing her in the conference room. Or when she'd shot the shit out of the clay targets and reminded me while I might have balls, she had a brass set of her own. This was a big fucking problem, especially since I couldn't have gotten rid of her any faster.

"Your man card's laminated and in Ella's wallet," I snarled.

"It sure as shit is." He was proud of it. He was also getting some on the regular, the fucker. And not just tail as he'd said, but he woke up to the woman he openly, and proudly, loved. I'd had a blast fucking with him when he and his Cinderella had gotten together. He'd been a total dumbass, not seeing how perfect Ella had been until it was almost too late.

I wasn't liking how the tables were turned.

Except they weren't. Rory was somewhere thirty-thousand feet over South Dakota by now. I wouldn't see her or her pussy again.

His eyes shifted over my shoulder and his smile slipped. "He's here."

East slid out of the booth and stood. I joined him, not wanting this fucker to get the upper hand. When I turned around, it was like I'd been sucker punched.

Holy fuck.

East was right.

I looked just like him.

South and his woman, Maisey, had been almost killed by a guy saying he was South's half-brother. Macon's *other* son. He and South looked nothing alike. Acted nothing alike since the man was a psycho and now in jail for a couple decades. Turned out, he wasn't Macon's kid anyway. Not that South would have given over any of Macon's inheritance to the guy because he'd already donated it all to charity.

We were used to this kind of shit, people wanting the Wainright money. I'd even fallen for it with Carrie and allowed a gold digger and social climber in my bed. My thoughts flicked to Rory and the fact that she was neither.

But this guy, my *father,* stood right in front of us.

We were built the same. Broad as a barn as North described me. Tall. Same square jaw. Same dark eyes. Although his hair was leaning toward gray, he still had all of it.

I was probably two inches taller and had thirty pounds on him. But there was zero question in my mind we shared the same genes. I should want to hug him. To go on a trail ride and catch up on lost time. Go fishing. Grill meat together. Bond.

Whatever the fuck real fathers and sons did. But looking at the man I knew he wasn't here to hand out old birthday cards. East knew it as well. We were well versed in people wanting to fuck us over for their own gain. Just wasn't used to it from a guy who looked like me.

"Son," he said, his voice rough like gravel.

My hackles rose. "You have no right to call me that," I murmured, leaning forward so no one else in the diner could hear.

If I had a relaxed look about me from getting laid, it was gone now.

I was taut like a bow string and ready to pick this guy up and toss him through a window.

Instead, I dropped into the side of the booth where East had been. No way I was sitting next to the man. I wanted to face him head on.

East slid in beside me.

The guy had no choice but to sit.

"Got a name?" I asked.

He was tan. Almost leathery. Lines like deep crevasses were on his cheeks, his forehead and at the corners of his eyes. The scent of stale cigarettes came off him in an invisible cloud. His clothing was clean, but not fancy. He looked like a typical sixty-year-old Montanan.

"Tank Million."

He had to be fucking kidding.

"Sounds like a porn star," East said. His hands were folded on the table, fingers interlocked.

Tank grinned and his yellow teeth made me look away. "Your momma sure liked my moves."

East growled and I was a second away from reaching across the table and slamming the guy's face down into the laminate. I didn't remember our mother, but I wouldn't have this asshole disrespect her. Even if they actually had been together. At least twice to make North and then me and East. Fuck. The coffee I'd had felt like acid in my stomach.

"On my birth certificate it says Travis," he continued. "Could've been on yours."

"What do you want?"

"Who says I want something?"

The waitress came around again and East waved her off with a flick of his fingers and a wink.

"You haven't been around in twenty-nine years. Why now? I'd say you want something," I said.

"Can't a father want to get to know his kids? It's never too late, right?"

I shifted. "Oh, it's definitely too fucking late."

The smile slipped from his face and a glint made his eyes go cold. "I had a deal with your daddy."

"I thought *you* were our daddy," I said, even the suggestion leaving a bad taste.

"Macon Wainright. The one on your birth certificate. *He* and I had a deal."

I shrugged. So did East at the same time. "So?"

"So the money didn't hit the bank on schedule and I just found out why. He's dead."

"That's not news to us," East said.

I looked to East. "We're done here. Let me out."

"You don't want me airing your family secrets, do you?"

I gritted my teeth but harnessed my anger into calmness. Everyone found that scarier than going Incredible Hulk. Besides, we had the upper hand here. This guy, regardless of DNA, only wanted one thing from us. Then he'd slither back under whatever rock he came from.

"Blackmail will put you in jail."

He held up his hands. "Just having a friendly conversation."

"Just talk, Tank. Tell us about the deal with Macon," East told him.

"Your daddy knew about me. How your mama was in love with me."

I wanted to tell him to quit with the *daddy* shit. Macon had never been our daddy. Not for one second. But I wanted him to keep on talking. To answer questions we'd been having since we found out Macon wasn't related.

"Your mother fell for me. My charm." He grinned. "Other things. But I didn't linger in town because I was on tour. Rodeo."

A traveling rodeo asshole. Great.

"When I came back by a few years later, let's just say she couldn't stay away, even married. Macon found us. Sent me off, but not before she told me the truth."

"What truth?" I asked. I wasn't going to make assumptions.

Tank's dark eyes flicked back and forth between ours, probably wondering if we even knew. Then a spark lit and I knew he was eager to be the one to reveal it.

"Macon fucked men. Not his wife. That's why she turned to me."

We waited and he squirmed a little. "We're waiting to find out why either of us give a shit," I said.

"Because Macon paid me every year to stay away. To keep your family's secrets to myself."

I leaned in, my knee bumping East's under the table.

"A real father wouldn't take money to stay away from his kids. He'd kill to be with them," I said.

"And family secrets?" East asked. "You think we give a shit if you tell?"

"You don't want your mother's good name tarnished, do you?" he countered.

"What would Macon's sexual status have anything to do with our mother?"

"He paid me to keep *his* secret, which was bad for her."

"He sure as fuck didn't pay you to stay quiet to

protect our mother. Especially since she died only four years after they married," I added.

"Then how about you four? Willing to protect your dead momma's good name?" He glared at him and stayed quiet. "Look, I didn't even know you were alive until the money didn't get into my bank this time. As long as the man paid, I didn't even think about him. Or your mother. Or their fucked up marriage. When the payment was missed, I did a little digging." He ran a hand over his face and eyed me. "Kitty and Macon Wainright had four kids. Four heirs. And lo and fucking behold, one of them looks *just like me.*"

He didn't even know he had kids? He didn't want us. He wanted money.

"You might be Mr. Million, but he and I—" I thumbed toward East. "—have billions. We can make *anything* go away. Including you."

His ruddy face blanched, but he came back around. "I'll go away if that deposit's in my account."

East climbed from the booth. I slid out after him. We looked down at the man who'd made us. No, he hadn't *made* us. He'd only been a sperm donor, just like we'd told South about Macon. We'd made ourselves and we'd turned out pretty fucking good considering.

"Do your worst, *Tank.* We don't give a shit," I said.

East tipped his hat and we left, knowing people couldn't be trusted. That we were always wanted for something. That making attachments only meant being screwed over in the end.

When I climbed in my truck, I picked up Rory's lingering scent. She was the only one who seemed to want one thing from me, and it wasn't money. Sex. She'd wanted my dick to satisfy her and nothing else.

Why did that make her perfect? And why did I miss her?

12

ORY

I GOT in late because of the time difference and a long layover in Chicago. After two days in Montana, the city sounds woke me. Had the trash truck always been so loud? Did cars always blast their music like that? Were people so grating and obnoxious? I'd never noticed any of it before but now it was irritating.

Looking out my office window—not the corner one but my small associates' space—I didn't see a tree or a blade of grass. I had to tilt my head back to see the blue sky, the sliver of it high between buildings.

For some crazy reason, standing on the tenth floor

of a midtown office building, I missed Montana. The peace. The quiet. And the man who lived there, even though he'd packed me up and shipped me off without more than a quick kiss because *his father* had shown up on his brother's doorstep.

Why was I so cranky? I wasn't prepared to purchase a piece of land and go all cowgirl. Winters in New York were gray and cold, but Montana? Could I even survive?

God, why was I thinking about making it through a winter out there?

It had been *three* days. West's orgasms hadn't been that great.

Okay, they had. The mark he'd left on my breast was fading, but not the memory of West and our time together. My pussy was still sore from the marathon fuck-fest we'd had. Had it only been twenty-four hours since his fingers had been inside me?

A knock on my open door had me turning.

"The pre-trial meeting for the Forbes case is at nine. The bi-laws rework for RF&G are due by eleven. Lunch with your mother's been on the books for two weeks."

My assistant, Jared, ran down my day without taking a breath. He didn't say hi. Didn't ask how my trip was. I'd been out of the office for four days—no one knew what the term *weekend* was—and he acted like I'd never left. Like I'd never gone somewhere so far out of my comfort zone that I felt... different.

"Then there's a client meeting with Nick Stevenson and..."

He droned on. This was our usual routine, him reading my calendar aloud every morning at seven-thirty. It ensured nothing was a surprise to me and that I didn't miss anything by only scanning my schedule on my computer screen.

"The Wainright contract was signed last night," he said. "You have a meeting with Rex Carlson from the engineering firm at two about next steps."

I blinked. "She signed it?"

Jared looked up from his tablet. Eyed me. Frowned. "Are you feeling all right?"

"Yes."

"It's been in your inbox since six last night."

"I was on a plane."

"Yes, but it's..." He looked at his tablet, then his watch. "Seven thirty-five. You didn't see it?"

I'd arrived at seven as usual, going through my morning motions, but I hadn't dug through all of my emails, all four hundred and sixty-two of them. Plus, there were the voice mails, interoffice memos.

"Haven't gotten to it yet," I replied, pointing to the

stack of papers in the middle of my desk. "Still digging out."

He nodded, looking confused.

"Give me an extra hour to get caught up," I told him, letting him know I'd be back to my normal driven self in sixty minutes.

His head went back and forth as he ran his finger over his tablet. "You don't have an extra hour."

"Right. Okay. So go." I dropped into my chair. "I'm back. I'm on it."

He nodded, then left.

A phone rang out in the central office area. An associate walked by in a crisp suit, not even taking the time to stick his head in and say hi.

There was no free time here.

Using my mouse, I scrolled through my inbox and found the email and attachment from the head lawyer at Wainright Holdings. The electronic document was there. Signature attached. Paul must have sent North the revised file and she'd reviewed it from home over the weekend.

I pictured her in the big house reading the latest version. Maybe Jed was beside her. I imagined her eating leftover egg casserole after she finalized the deal. Maybe even went for a swim in the pool I'd walked past. Gone for a horseback ride. Made love.

"Heard the deal was signed."

Startled, I looked up at my father in the doorway. He always wore black suits. Never navy. White shirt. The only thing that deviated was the color of his tie. Gray, blue or silver.

"That's right," I replied, smiling. Exhilarated that it was done.

"That will make Rex happy, but that's old news."

Um, what? I'd known for all of a few minutes.

"Six new clients were signed while you were gone," he continued. "Mike tackled them in your absence."

"I was with North Wainright," I reminded. I mentioned exactly what West had told me, that being with a billable client would hold up.

He waved his hand in the air, his signet ring glinting. "Focusing on one client doesn't run a business."

My heart kicked up a notch and I felt the usual flare of shame and disappointment. "I went to Montana for a client. I didn't go off to Cancun for spring break."

He frowned. We looked a fair amount alike. Same dark hair. Eyes. Except I was petite like my mother. Everyone said we had the same mannerisms, the same drive.

"You can't hit the ball out of the park if you're not at home plate swinging," he reminded.

Fuck. I'd been sexing it up with West. I *knew* it would come back to bite me in the ass!

"The Wainright deal is signed. I'd say we hit it out of the park. It's big." *Big enough for me to finally make partner.*

I was waiting for him to be pleased. To make *him* happy, not just Rex the client. I'd worked my ass off for months negotiating the whole thing. I'd flown to Montana. Rode a horse. Rode a cowboy.

"I can't hand hold you, Rory."

Hand hold me? I was just looking for kudos for good work. A pat on the back. A *good job*. Except, that clearly wasn't coming, all because I'd lingered out of the office. It had never come and I wasn't sure why I was expecting it now. I swallowed down the familiar pill of disappointment. "I understand. I have a meeting at nine I need to prepare for."

He nodded, then left. No hello, no goodbye. He was in boss mode, not father mode. Not that I ever remember him acting like a father. Here, at the office, I was another associate. Nothing more. I rarely went to my parents' apartment, only meeting them out for dinner or at a function. Then, my father was *always* on, networking and ready to snag someone needing legal help.

I settled into my work, trying to ignore my growing irritation with... everything.

Work was where I was able to focus, to not think about how my father hadn't mentioned the partner spot. To distract myself from any feelings I might have. Because a lawyer was neutral, a Switzerland of sorts for a client. We didn't state our case with personal emotions, but with facts and arguments.

My cell pinged and I realized an hour had passed. I grabbed it off the desk, read the display.

Unknown caller, but had the Montana area code which had become familiar.

Heard my sister signed the contract. Congrats.

My skin flushed and I had to take a deep breath. I felt like a seventh grader when a cute boy looked my way.

West?

Know a lot of people whose sister signs contracts?

I smirked.

Yeah, well. I lost out on other clients because I wasn't here.

I sounded like a seventh grader missing out on hanging out at the mall with friends.

Let me guess, Mansplain Mike got them.

His term made the corner of my mouth twitch. *Yes.*

Let him suffer under the load. I'm guessing he didn't get fucked this weekend.

I didn't want to think about Mike having sex, but West did have a point.

There will be others. Never-ending legal battles need to be conquered.

I could have been working, West.

Yeah, you could have. But you weren't.

I huffed and let my fingers fly. *Now I'm paying the price.*

Cranky, kitten?

I tossed my hands in the air and wanted to scream.

I'm allowed to have feelings. Including cranky ones.

Pretty fucking angry for being in your fancy new office.

I looked around the small one I'd had for years. It barely had room for a desk and a chair. Definitely not a floor plant.

No new office.

You didn't get partner?

Not yet.

What's your daddy waiting for?

That was a good question. I juggled so many balls as it was. Being away, I'd missed adding six more in the air. Next up was going to be chainsaws.

What are you waiting for?

He added that and I stared at the words. What was

I waiting for? For my father to congratulate me for a job well done with a corner office with a huge bow on the door? I didn't know how to respond because I didn't know what to do. I couldn't go to my father and remind him that I should be partner now because all he'd do is tell me he gave no favoritism because we were related. I'd done that once and I'd been humiliated. But then, was he constantly drawing a new line in the sand every time I reached the last one. I had no answer, so I didn't reply.

You closed the deal, kitten. Way to go. North's a hard ass and would only sign something solid.

His praise felt good and I couldn't help but smile. It hadn't come from my dad and I knew none of the other associates would take me out for drinks. Jared hadn't even said good job. There wasn't any "rising tides raising all boats" around here. I hadn't left my desk since I arrived this morning but I could imagine what the other associates had taken on while I'd been away.

It's your patents everyone wants.

I reminded him with my latest text he should be proud of himself.

It's nothing more than tinkering.

Nothing more than... I sputtered. His inventions were revolutionizing water usage to crops and animals on farms and ranches. He wasn't building something with Legos. While he might do all that complicated thinking in a small room in his stable, it didn't make him any less of a genius.

How was the meeting with your father? I couldn't believe I'd almost forgotten. He'd been really upset about it.

It went.

What the hell did that mean?

Is he your dad?

Absolutely.

That's great.

Jared stuck his head in. "Problem at the court-house. Group meeting starting in five."

I rolled my eyes. Sighed.

Gotta go. Tell me more about him later.

Be a good girl, kitten.

13

EST

"I PULLED up everything I could about him," Jed said. He tossed a stack of papers on the kitchen counter. North's chef had made Mexican for dinner, but we hadn't gotten to it yet.

After our meeting with Tank the day before, I'd called Jed on the ride home. I'd had nothing to share about the guy other than his name, general age and that he used to work the rodeo circuit. I had nothing else.

Jed had hung up and got to work—even though it was a Sunday this impacted his woman—while I got nice and sweaty and exhausted tossing hay bales, then saddled up my horse and went for a ride until sunset. I'd tried to avoid thinking about Tank... and Rory. I hadn't been able to get either out of my head.

Tank because he was a thorn in my side and Rory because she was... stuck there.

It had taken Jed a day, but he'd called us all together at the big house because he had something. It seemed his connections and background were consistently useful. Tossing money around was one thing, but access to the FBI's databases was another. Him being part of the family meant less non-disclosure agreements. Less who knew what the fuck we were up to.

We'd convened in front of the taco buffet. East and Ella had driven up from Bozeman for this because it was a big fucking deal. Neither had summer classes. Ella had graduated in May and her master's program didn't start until next month. East was on break so they were flexible. And East felt as I did.

Angry and pissed. We'd sat across the booth from our *father* and all the man had cared about was money. Not us.

South and Maisey arrived a little while ago and the helicopter had just landed bringing North and Jed back from the corporate office. North hadn't changed because I was sure she was as anxious as we were. I didn't want to wait for her to put on sweats for the rundown. While Jed probably shared some details on the trip back, I was sure he wanted to tell all of us at once.

I wasn't the only one tense. Maisey was holding South's hand and East was sticking close to Ella.

Now was different than other times people had come after us for our money. North would sic the corporate lawyers on them and we'd never see them again. But this? There really wasn't any doubt with Tank being related since I looked exactly like him.

It was really fucking weird knowing what I was going to look like in thirty years.

"Travis 'Tank' Million, born 1962 in Minot, North Dakota," Jed began, reading from the top paper in his pile.

"His name really is Million?" Maisey asked. She'd grabbed a glass from the cabinet and was on her way to fill it at the fridge water dispenser, but she'd paused to ask.

"Fucking ironic," I muttered.

Jed nodded. "It is. The details of schooling, parents and all that are in there." He pointed to the pile. "But I'll jump to the more important parts, and what took me a while to dig up."

His dark eyes slid over each of us. We were circled around the island, Ella sitting in one of the bar stools, East's hand on her shoulder.

"He was in the pro rodeo circuit for almost ten years," Jed continued after picking up another page. "I did some math using North's birth date and the timing of when he'd have been in the area."

Meaning when Tank and our mother had crossed paths long enough to have sex and make North.

"He was here for about a month. Did the county rodeo circuit. His name's on the participant lists." Jed ran a hand over his beard and glanced at North.

"A month's long enough," North added. She picked up a page with a photo and passed it to Maisey.

"Wow, he was handsome." Maisey stopped studying the image and turned her head my way. "I can't get over how much you two look alike."

I didn't need a picture to agree with her.

"You calling me handsome?" I teased with a wink.

South slung an arm around Maisey's shoulder in a possessive gesture.

"All you boys are handsome," she replied. "You don't need me telling you that because your egos are big enough already."

"I've got something big for you," South murmured in her ear.

Maisey flushed and giggled. "Later," she whispered.

I'd never seen Jed roll his eyes, but I had a feeling he wanted to at the fact that South was thinking about fucking his woman right about now. Then, of course, this wasn't his dad. His dad was Macon, and he was dead. Unless he was a ghost, he wasn't coming back to haunt him. My thought wasn't fair though. South was just invested in this mess as the rest of us. We'd learned long ago it didn't matter who'd fathered us, except when he was fucking with us.

Jed pushed on. "Records from the rodeo organization show Tank competing—and winning—in events the rest of the summer and throughout the fall elsewhere in the country."

"Meaning he came, he fucked, he left," East added.

Jed glanced across the counter at my twin. "Yes."

"So Mom had a fling with a rodeo guy, got pregnant and he left," North summed up. "All before she met Macon."

"Well, I can't say if she and Macon hadn't met," Jed murmured. "But they married while she was pregnant with you. So it had to have been quick dating."

"A whirlwind romance?" Ella asked, glancing up at East.

"Macon being romantic? Impossible," he muttered.

Not a chance.

We knew Mom had been pregnant before she wed. But we'd always thought she and Macon had gotten to their wedding night—like most people these days—well before the wedding. That was before we'd learned of Macon being gay. We would have assumed then that they never had sex and that all four of us were someone else's, except South's DNA proved he hadn't been delivered by a stork.

"I'm fucking eating," East grumbled, leaving Ella and going around the island. "I'm not letting Tank ruin my dinner." He grabbed a plate and started to build some tacos.

"When did the payments start?" I asked Jed but kept my eyes on East's plate and how it was filling up fast. "I mean, why would Macon pay Tank off from the start? Obviously, he and Mom got back together at least one more time to make us." I pointed between me and East.

I wasn't going to think about Tank fucking, but there was no way around it.

I glanced at East. His jaw clenched and I knew he was imagining the same thing.

"Statements show annual wires of a hundred thousand dollars to a bank in Boise in Tank's name," Jed stated. "They started the year you two were born and were consistent every July since."

"Meaning Macon knew that Mom was having an affair," East added. "Except Tank said he didn't even know he had any kids until he saw a picture of West well *after* Macon had died. In the past few weeks. He only paid the Wainrights any attention when the annual payment stopped. Obviously, he knows I'm his since we're twins, but based on what he said yesterday at the diner, I doubt he knows he has a daughter, too."

Jed gave a slight shrug because he'd been through all of this for the past year. He loved North no matter who her father was. "I want to know if the payoff was to keep Macon's secret or to get Tank to stay away. The only one alive to ask is Tank."

"I can change that," East said, then took a huge bite of guac covered taco.

I could help him. There was plenty of land to bury a body.

Jed didn't even blink at East's implication of making Tank dead.

"He's not going away," I said. "Not now that he can carry on the payments with the next generation."

"You think he'd... blackmail his own kids for money?" Maisey asked. She had a twin of her own.

Identical. I'd met the crazy woman and Maisey was *very* familiar with a fucked up family.

"Wouldn't put it past anyone tied to us," South told her.

North shook her head. "You're right, West. He'll be back. But if Macon paid him to stay away *and* quiet, it doesn't matter any longer. He has no hold over us. Not that I want him around even if he is our father," she added. "Besides, we can have him arrested for blackmail."

"There's no proof to do so. Yet," Jed replied.

I held up my hand. "Wait. We know he's our father." I pointed again to East. "The guy didn't know he had kids. Meaning he might not be your father, North."

East shook his head. "No, if he's ours, he's hers too. Remember, the DNA showed the same parents for all three of us."

Shit, he was right. I forgot about that.

North took a deep breath. "Still. Didn't they teach condom use back then?"

"Based on the rodeo schedule and your birthday, even if we didn't have the DNA report, it makes sense that he's your father too," Jed clarified. "My guess? Your mom hooked up with a hot rodeo guy. Got pregnant and he left town, moving on to the next competition. Your mom found herself pregnant with a now long-gone sperm donor and didn't feel like she had a choice about marrying Macon."

"This was thirty years ago, not one hundred," South reminded. "She wasn't going to be shunned or tossed out for getting knocked up. Whatever. I mean, the money was hers."

The *billion* in Billionaire Ranch came from our mother's family. Macon only married into it.

"So you think he came back around again for another year of rodeo events and Mom tracked him down?" North asked, looking to Jed. "Had another fling? Didn't tell him about North, or the fact that she had South with Macon?"

Jed shrugged. "From what East and West said, the guy didn't sound like he was in love with your mom. It makes sense."

"So they go at it his second time in the area and she's Miss Fertile and gets pregnant again?" North asked. I couldn't tell if she was getting frustrated with our mother or Tank's easy-come, easy-go attitude.

I wasn't one to talk. I'd just had a fling with a lawyer from New York. I *could* see desire clouding judgment. And if Rory came back to Montana, I'd definitely have another spin.

Reaching out, Jed cupped her jaw. "Princess, I don't have those answers."

"Not that I want to think about your parents having sex, but if Macon wasn't satisfying her, could you blame her for looking elsewhere?" Ella asked. She'd grown up in foster care, so she didn't have any parents to imagine in that way.

No one said anything, because it was definitely a possibility.

"Fine. Mom had needs back then," East said finally, spreading sour cream across the top of his remaining tacos. "Now? We don't care about keeping Macon's secret and we can get a restraining order against Tank if he comes back."

I was following. Listening quietly. Considering.

I had no answers. Just knew that it didn't matter if Macon or Tank was our father. All four of us had *asshole* in our blood. I tried to steer clear of trouble. Of problems. I loved a quiet, simple life. I kept my head down and had dodged most of Macon's shit once I'd gone away to college, even after settling on my own ranch down the road. I'd been dumb with Carrie, but had learned my lesson.

But this time, trouble had come to me and in the form of my own father. Like South had wondered when we'd learned about his DNA matching Macon's, maybe we were tainted. I'd talked him out of those stupid thoughts when it had been his sperm donor we'd been talking about. But now? When it was mine and I looked like the bastard? I might have been wrong.

East knew what he was saying wasn't going to cut it. What man, who got paid six figures every year for doing nothing except staying out of the area, would give that up?

"There's nothing we can do until he shows his face again," South added. He kissed the top of Maisey's head and grabbed a plate, passed it to her, then grabbed one for himself. She stood and followed behind him to build tacos from the spread.

"Speaking of not wanting someone around," North continued, then waggled her eyebrows at me. "You ditched Rory pretty fast."

Maisey grabbed silverware and moved to the table. South followed. "Who's Rory?" she asked.

I went to the food to give me something to do instead of standing there like an idiot. Grabbing a plate, I got busy as I told North off. "You are a terrible matchmaker."

"Matchmaker?" Ella asked, snagging a nacho chip off of East's plate. Her eyebrows waggled and she looked like she was settling in for a gossip session. "With West?"

"She had me pick up a lawyer at the airport," I explained, loading carnitas onto a row of street-sized tortillas on my plate. "A *female* lawyer."

Ella smiled and glanced at North. "And?"

"And they had sex," North replied.

I set my plate down and stared at my sister. South and Maisey laughed from the table.

"How the hell do you know that?" I barked.

North grinned and set her hands on her hips. "Besides the look on your face right now?"

Fuck me. I could feel that my cheeks were hot. "Yeah, besides that."

Jed grinned. East slapped me on the back. "Welcome to the club, asshole."

"Club? It was a fling."

"It's obvious," North said, ignoring East.

Unless she saw us together somehow, I wasn't sure how it was obvious.

I continued to stare, so she finally explained.

"When you showed up to the meeting, introductions were made. You two pretended you didn't know each other."

I thought back but all I could remember was how stunned I'd been to see her there.

"You asked me to join the meeting because of Rory?" I looked to North, growled.

North raised a brow, gave me a look that screamed I was an idiot. "So clueless," she muttered, then continued. "I knew you picked her up from the airport because... I sent you. So if nothing had happened after you collected her, you'd have said, *good to see you again* or something like that at the meeting. Instead, you introduced yourselves. Total fake out. The heat bouncing between the two of you could have melted January snow and you guys did a horrible job of ignoring each other during the meeting."

I closed my eyes and gritted my teeth. Fuck, she was right.

"It was a fling," I repeated, finally looking to North. "She's back in New York."

"She's perfect for you," she countered. "I've been working with her for months over the phone and email and she's great."

I raised my eyebrows and stared.

"Rory's a woman West slept with, but *who* is she and why is she in New York?" Maisey whispered to South. He leaned in and probably gave her the details, but I couldn't hear.

"Perfect?" I snapped. "She's focused on making partner and has no interest in a cowboy."

North looked to Jed. "Worked for us. I was focused on my work, not this hot cowboy and look where I am now."

I sighed. "Whatever. I'm not going for a woman like her again."

East put his third taco down and frowned. "Again? Are you talking about that girl from college? What was her name? Caren? Carla?"

"Carrie," I said, growling.

"Jesus, that was years ago. Tell me you haven't been a monk since then."

I rolled my eyes. I wasn't a fucking monk, but I didn't do relationships. The only people I cared about were the people in this room and they all knew how fucked up I was. Or maybe they didn't.

"Does Rory want your money?" South asked.

"Hell, no." I turned to face him. "She's like a dog with a bone about her career. It gets pretty crowded in bed with a career between us."

When I realized what I'd said, I glanced at North.

"Sorry," I bit out. Even though she'd fixed me up— fucking hell—I wouldn't hurt her feelings intentionally. Be pissed at her, sure. But not intentionally cruel. Macon had done that enough.

She held up her hand. "You're right. That's why I

don't work nights or weekends any longer. Jed likes me all to myself."

"That's right, princess."

"Maybe she's hiding like I was," North added. "Pushing herself because if she stopped, she'd see how fucked up her life is."

Jed pulled North into his side and kissed the top of her head.

After Macon died and Jed did his thing, North had changed. For the better. But Rory? Was she using work as a bandage on her life? If she pulled it off, would she bleed out?

I had to wonder if I'd made things better for her, if only for a little while, or worse.

I should leave Rory alone. She'd made it clear I was a fling. I should be thrilled to get laid and have no strings. Except I'd made her submit, to wind all her shit down and I'd caught a glimpse of the real Rory Sullivan. The one without the power suit and cell phone. Without the eye on the corner office. All she'd eyed was my dick. And she'd liked it. And the rest of me.

I wanted more of *that* version of Rory. I had to wonder if Rory wanted that version of herself too.

14

ORY

"DID you pick out a dress for the gala?" my mother asked. She lifted her dirty martini and took a sip. A waiter passed and she raised the almost-empty glass to signal for another. She wasn't a lush, but she always had a few drinks with dinner.

We were at her favorite restaurant, Chez Manu. My father was on his cell and we were waiting on my brother who was late... again, for something medical and life saving. While I worked with my father, it had been my mother who'd dragged me from my desk for this impromptu meal. If my father was here, then I could be without being considered a slacker.

"Not yet. I was going to go later this week," I replied.

The ambiance was all dark wood and brass. The lighting muted. But it was crowded and noisy, but that was how my parents liked it. The ability to see and be seen.

"Later this week?" she countered, eyes wide.

"It's a dress, Mother. I've been busy at work."

Our eyes slid to my father, who held up his finger. I wasn't sure if it was to tell us he would only be a minute or as a warning for us not to interrupt him on his cell. We'd shared a car from the office and we'd spoken only about work stuff until he got a call he'd taken as we'd entered the restaurant, led to the table and even as he ordered a drink.

I thought of West and how he'd asked me if my cell was glued to my hand. I wasn't holding mine, but it was on the table beside my silverware. My mother's, with the sparkly case, was in the same spot in front of her.

Now I could see how ridiculous I'd been taking the call from Mike while West had been breathing on my pussy. I was just like my father. No, worse. A gorgeous cowboy on his knees and I'd taken a phone call.

God, I had been an idiot.

My brother appeared, weaving through the crowd. "The surgery ran long." He leaned down and kissed my mother's cheek, then settled into the empty spot.

Matthew and I looked alike, although between med school, years of residency and other training programs, he was graying early. He gave me a nod and waved down the waiter.

My father separated himself from his call and dropped the overworked cell on the table. He smiled at Matthew, clearly pleased to see him. "How'd that craniotomy go?"

"Which one?" Matthew countered.

My dad laughed, drawing eyes from those at nearby tables.

"Any of them."

Matthew sniffed and adjusted his tie. "They were all successful."

Of course, they were.

"Look at that, Rory," my mother preened. "Your brother saving lives."

"Youngest neurosurgeon fellow in New York," my father reminded, although it wasn't necessary as I knew that *all* too well.

Yes, I was well aware of this and how proud they were of Matthew.

The waiter came over, thankfully, and kept me from praising him for something we already knew. Matthew was perfect. Matthew was smart. Successful. Had a penis.

"How's Hadley?" Mother asked him.

"She's leading the benefit next month for the children's cancer ward," Matthew replied. "She told me to tell you that she found the perfect shoes to match her dress for the gala."

"Shoes?" my father scoffed. "Women's work."

"Women's work is also closing a deal with Wainright Holdings," I prompted.

My father gave a negligent wave. "It's not brain surgery."

No, it wasn't. So I wasn't a fancy doctor, but neither was he.

My cell lit up and I nabbed it like a lifeline out of this insanity. My cheeks went hot seeing West's name. I pulled the phone close as if I couldn't read far away instead of the fact that I didn't want anyone to see the screen. No one cared that I used my phone at the table.

I wonder if your desk chair has an ass groove. I mean, you're in it more than your bed.

I pursed my lips, trying not to smile. The conversation at the table went on without me.

Probably.

I'd never thought about it before, but he was right. I slept about six hours and worked at least twelve.

Did you eat dinner, kitten?

I'm at dinner now.

Outside of your office?

In a restaurant.

Did you escape through a vent in the wall or were you paroled?

I rolled my eyes, then glanced at my mother. She had her hand on Matthew's wrist and smiling adoringly at whatever he was droning on about. Something about lasers and brain waves.

Supervised release. I'm with my parents and brother.

That bad?

"Rory, did you hear? Matthew's going to ask Hadley to marry him this weekend. Isn't that wonderful? Think of how fun it will be to plan a wedding!" My mother practically clapped her hands together in glee—while holding her drink.

I nodded.

"Someday we'll plan yours," she said longingly, as if all that mattered was the event.

"Work keeps me busy," I replied.

My dad smirked. "Until you find a man."

I whipped my head in his direction. "I'm up for partner."

He took a sip of his drink. "It's pretty hard to run a firm when you're making babies."

I frowned. "Who said anything about having a baby?"

He pointed to my mother. "She wants grandchildren."

I hadn't thought much about having kids. Maybe someday, but so far only considered it in a tangential way. Just like the guy I'd make them with.

My mother looked at me longingly, as if my uterus were the key to her happiness. She hadn't been all that hands on when I was a kid, so I was surprised she wanted drooling, crying mini-people around her again.

"At least find a man so you can settle down, Rory."

My mother's words were not new, but my dad's were.

"What are you saying, Dad? That I should quit to have kids so Mom will be happy?"

"That's what women do."

I sat up straight and angled myself toward my father. "You wouldn't be saying any of this if I were a man." I was right. If I had a penis everything would be different. "You do realize you're headed into sexual harassment territory."

He looked like he had heartburn. "Sexual harassment? Why would I worry about that when you're my daughter."

"Only a woman would talk like you do, using your gender to be angry at the reality of what Dad is saying," my brother added.

I looked to my brother. Blinked. Then again.

"That's because only *women* are told they shouldn't expect success in the workplace because they have a uterus, which they might not even choose to use."

My blood was pumping and I couldn't believe we were having this conversation.

"Semantics," Dad said.

I remembered West had said that details mattered. That only worked if people saw eye-to-eye, which of course no one ever did. That was why I was a fucking lawyer.

"I'm also an associate in the firm you run who's making partner," I reminded.

He huffed. "That's yet to be seen. Mike's taking on six clients right now on top of having gone to Montana."

It was the second time he'd said that to me today.

"Are you kidding me?"

Mike would get the promotion solely because he showed up in Montana, fumbled for an hour meeting? That he'd only gotten those extra clients solely because North had thought he was a dud and sent him packing? Did my father have any idea how much of a dumbass the guy was? And *he* was going to be partner?

My cell vibrated in my hand. I glanced down. I felt hot all over. My head spun from what had just gone down. My mother, clearly moving on from the whole grandchildren thing, tittered at something Matthew said. Maybe he was promising her he'd knock Hadley up later tonight. He sucked up every bit of her fawning and ignored me.

My father signaled for the waiter. He came over and my mother gave her order.

I glanced at the screen. *Kitten. Talk to me.*

Why are you texting me? I typed. *It was a fling, West. We agreed it was nothing more.*

I have no fucking clue.

Well, that made me feel better.

So tell me. What's a dinner like with parents?

He wanted to know? I glanced up, looked at the trio I shared blood with. Yeah, they made me so mad, my fingers were shaking as I typed. *Horrible. Were my parents always so shallow and demeaning?*

I hit send before I thought about what I wrote.

Excuse yourself and go to the bathroom.

What?

You read it right. Go.

I stood and my family looked up at me. My father with his drink in hand. My mother nibbled on the pearl onion at the end of a toothpick. My brother tugged on his shirt cuffs. They were so self-involved I was surprised they noticed I stood up. "Ladies room," I whispered.

"The waiter is here to order," my mother complained as the man hovered at her right.

I looked to the stoic man. I was sure he'd seen crazier families than mine. "The salmon, please."

He nodded and I made my escape.

OK. I wrote it once I entered the opulent bathroom.

A few seconds later, my cell rang. I startled, then answered it.

"West," I breathed.

"What's going on with your parents, kitten?"

God, his voice. All deep and rumbly and... interested.

"You never told me about the meeting with the man who showed up at East's house. Is he your dad?"

"This call isn't about me, kitten. Your parents upset you."

"Why do you care?" I asked, then winced. West had been down for a good time, not the long haul. Neither was I. That didn't mean he wasn't a decent guy. "Sorry."

I rubbed my forehead and stared down at my heels. They were black and tall and had a little strap that ran over my ankle. They paired well with my black dress with the white Peter Pan collar.

"Tell me."

There wasn't anyone else to talk to and going back out there right now was *not* something I was eager to do.

So I talked. "Nothing new. They're being themselves." I wasn't going to rehash the whole babymaker thing with West because it would probably make him panic even though I was on the pill *and* we'd used condoms.

He grunted, as if in understanding. I knew from my research his mother had died when he was very young and he and his siblings had lived with Macon who I, and everyone else in the world, assumed was their father. The way West had closed up when I'd once mentioned Macon, it didn't seem like he'd gotten on with the man.

"You work all day?" he asked, breaking me from my thoughts.

I frowned, but he couldn't see it. "Of course."

"You working tonight?"

"From home."

"You've put in twelve hours so far."

I sighed. "What else is new?"

"Don't sass me, kitten. If I was there, I'd take you over my knee."

A whimper escaped before I could stifle it. The idea of him tugging me over his sturdy thighs, my ass in the air for him to spank...

"Oh, kitten. You like that idea?"

I didn't say anything, just spun on my heel and faced the wall. I'd been uninhibited with him, tossing my insecurities and been brave enough to proposition him. Even though he was almost two thousand miles away, shame filled me that he'd caught on to a kink, one I hadn't even known I had until now.

"Time to give me control," he murmured, his voice going deeper in that deliciously dark way.

"What?"

"Do what I tell you."

"Now?" I glanced around the empty bathroom.

"Now. You don't have to think about work. Or your family. Just listen to my words and obey."

"I don't—"

"Yes, you do," he cut off. "Go into one of the stalls."

I didn't move.

"Now, kitten." I had no idea how he knew I hadn't done anything. "Or you won't get your reward for being a good girl."

Oh shit. I loved it when he said that.

There were three stalls, all empty, and I went to the furthest one, locked the door.

"Okay," I whispered.

"You wearing one of those dresses?"

I didn't know what *those* meant, but I told him yes.

"Pull it up to your waist."

"You can't be serious," I hissed.

"You're going to come before you go back out to dinner with your parents. You can do it right away like a good girl or we can argue for a few minutes first. Either way, that clit's getting rubbed and you're getting off."

"Oh my God," I whispered.

"Now get your hand in those panties."

With one hand holding the cell, I tugged up the hem of my dress with the other so it gathered at my waist. I had no idea why I was nervous and a little embarrassed. This was exactly what people did in a bathroom stall–lifting skirts. Except I'd never masturbated before in one.

"What if someone comes in?" I whispered.

"Then you better be quiet."

I slipped my hand down the front of my silk thong. I was wet. It was West being bossy, even from far away, that made me that way.

I whimpered again, then bit my lip, when I circled my fingers over my clit.

"Just like that, kitten. Imagine it's my fingers on you. My mouth."

"West," I whispered. I'd never had phone sex before and never imagined doing something like this in my mother's favorite restaurant.

But the stall made it feel like a weird cocoon where it was just me and West. Alone.

"I bet you're dripping, aren't you?"

"Mmhmm," I breathed as I worked myself harder and faster.

"Such a good girl fingering yourself."

And I came. Ridiculously fast. Just like that because he was a dirty talker and being his good girl got me off so good. My pussy pulsed, my muscles clenched. It was incredible. Fuck, it was the most amazing orgasm, except I was empty. I missed West's thick cock. His hard body over me. The rough pounding.

"Holy fuck, kitten. That was hot."

I leaned my head against the cool metal wall, eyes

closed. I tried to catch my breath and calm my racing heart. "Uh huh."

"You go back out there and remember why your panties are all wet. Why your pussy's throbbing. You can do anything, kitten. Even handle your crazy family."

 EST

HOW'S YOUR LATEST INVENTION?

How's your latest meeting? I countered easily.

I shouldn't have shown Rory my work room or what I'd been working on, but I had. She'd been interested. Impressed. It didn't matter though. It was only tinkering, to get the ideas out of my head and make them real. What happened after they were finished didn't matter. I handed them off to North to deal with.

I was in the stable, just finished laying out new straw in one of the horse stalls and seeing the text, the one Rory had sent on her own, made me feel... good.

It'd been two days since the phone sex. I'd listened to her get off—in a fucking restaurant bathroom—and then had to shower and rub one out. No way could I survive with a hard dick and blue balls after listening to her stifled whimpers of pleasure.

Which one? I have probably five a day.

I set the pitchfork against the wall to type. *I thought you got partner if North signed the contract.*

Before she got her fingers on her clit, she'd let me know she hadn't gotten the partner spot. But it had been two days since then.

It took her a bit to respond and I'd turned the lights out in the stable and headed toward the house. What the hell was going on over there?

I did too.

I didn't know her father, but I wanted to go and have a word with him for stringing his daughter along. Why hadn't she been promoted?

I was halfway across the field and stopped mid-stride. Oh shit.

Did Mike the loser get it? My fingers were big for the cell, but I did okay with texting.

No one got it. Yet.

I breathed a touch easier because the thought of that moron getting the spot Rory had rightfully earned pissed me off.

Except that was what happened when you stuck yourself out there. Strived for a goal that someone could fuck with. Rory was promised the position from her father, so she had every right to think it would come through. Not all parents were like mine, although her update had me knowing Mr. Sullivan was stringing her along.

But why? If she'd closed the deal, why fuck with her?

I came in through the back door, dropped onto the bench I kept there to tug off my dirty boots.

Not that I'd tell Rory any of those thoughts. Hell, no. It was her dream and I wanted her to have it.

Funny, I had billions and this was one thing I couldn't give to her.

I'd been the one with the patent she'd negotiated for and I *still* hadn't been able to help.

Off to a meeting.

You need an orgasm before you go in?

The answer is yes, I always need one. But there's no time.

No time to get off? I had to solve that problem. Later. For now, I needed some lunch... and to rub one out. Again.

RORY

Is the man you met really your father?

I look just like him. So yes.

That's great! Wait. Is it?

I bit my lip and stared at the screen. I had no idea what the hell I was doing with West. Texting and phone sex? It wasn't a relationship. It wasn't anything. Except we weren't arguing. I was learning things about him and he was getting me off.

It was after ten and I'd just gotten home from the office. I'd picked up my usual Thai order and poured a glass of wine to go with it.

I didn't have time to analyze whatever we were doing that closely so I was going with it. He wasn't in New York. Wasn't related. He was oddly safe to talk to because he had nothing invested in me. The same in return. I wasn't after West's money. Or much of his time. Pretty much, I wanted him to text me and be a little bossy and call me good girl and... make me feel better.

Because having a long-distance phone relationship with him seemed healthy.

Which was completely ridiculous.

No.

I opened the lid on the Pad See Ewe and stuck my fork into the steaming noodles.

Instead of texting, I pressed the little phone icon, then speaker.

"Don't you ever sleep?" he said instead of a simple hello. Or my name. Or *kitten.*

"What's the situation with your dad?"

I heard his sigh through the phone.

"If you don't tell me, I'm not doing phone sex with you anymore," I added.

"You sure you want to use that threat, kitten? You're the one who's going to suffer," he countered.

True. So fucking true. My pussy clenched remembering how good it had been. The time at the restaurant I'd been able to rejoin my family and get through the meal, not caring that I could never keep up with Matthew.

"I'm the one who makes the deals," I reminded, then took a sip of my wine. "Maybe I'm being strategic."

"Okay, kitten. I tell you and then I get you off."

"West," I replied.

"Take it or leave it."

"I'll take it."

"Good girl." He sighed. I inwardly glowed. "You know Macon's not my father. You learned that when you were here, but we only found out after he died last year. Except South's his kid. The three of us, we didn't know who our sperm donor was until Sunday morning when the man showed up on East's doorstep."

"Why then?" I wondered.

"Macon had been paying him annually to stay away. Or some other reason we haven't figured out yet. Macon died and the money stopped. Million wants more."

"Million?"

"His name is Travis Million."

"Seriously?" I took another sip of wine. Listening to West and the crisp alcohol were a relaxing combination.

"Yes."

"Are you going to pay him?"

There was a pause and I could imagine him shrugging. "We told him to fuck off. We made it really clear we had no intention of giving him a dime. He hasn't been back around yet, but we expect him to do something. They always do."

I knew a relaxed, at ease West. Usually it was when his dick was hard and we were naked. This wasn't him. I couldn't miss how he sounded angry and even a little frustrated. But I couldn't blame him. He hadn't liked

Macon Wainright and this guy sounded like a money-grubbing asshole.

"I'm sorry," I said.

"For what, kitten? You didn't fuck our mother."

Yeah, he wasn't happy.

"For having two shitty fathers."

"You make partner yet?"

The question threw me. "No."

"Then you've got a shitty one too."

"He's not shitty," I countered quickly. "He's—"

"An asshole."

I didn't like West saying that. He hadn't met my father. Didn't understand the kind of businessman, the kind of lawyer, he was. Rural Montana wasn't New York. One had to have rough edges to survive. "West."

"He said you'd get partner if you closed the deal with North, right?"

"Yes."

"Are you partner?"

I pursed my lips as I poked at the noodles.

"Why stay at the firm if they're going to string you along? There are lots of lawyer jobs out there."

"This has been my dream."

"Dreams change, kitten."

"What about you?" I countered. "What about your dreams?"

"I'm living the exact life I want."

"Really? Don't you want to be known for how your ideas are revolutionizing ranching?"

"Don't you want the same thing? To be seen for your accomplishments? The difference is, I'm not trying to prove myself to anyone."

Was I trying to prove myself to my dad? Hell, yes I was. I hadn't been doing anything else with my life since I was little. Trying to be seen while growing up behind Matthew.

"I can't just walk away now," I snapped.

"Why the hell not? Just quit. You'd be scooped up in a second. Or you could work for yourself. Hell, you could work for North."

I laughed. Me, work for Wainright Holdings. I ran a hand over my face. God, I was tired.

"Right. Like you'd want me in Montana." I sighed, a little disappointed I was probably right in my statement and a little confused as to why I was actually disappointed. "I need to eat. Then go to bed. I have to go shopping tomorrow for a dress. I'd rather face a misogynistic judge than the fancy dress section of Neimans."

"Dress for what?"

"My mother is chair of a charity gala. It's next weekend. The Sullivans have bought a table."

"You love wearing dresses and ridiculous heels."

"I do, but this one's different. This is for the annual gala that I'm being forced to attend. Matthew—my brother—is going to be showing off his new fiancée. My father will drink and schmooze anyone with a bank account with seven zeroes. Mike Spain will be following behind like an eager puppy. I'll have to stand with the two of them. Plus, my mother will be pushing Mark Rutherford at me."

"Who the hell is Mark Rutherford?" he snarled.

"If my mother has her way, the man I'm going to marry and make her grandchildren with."

He swore under his breath.

"When is this *gala*?" he asked, spitting out the last as if it were foul tasting. I couldn't picture him networking and social climbing at a function like that, although he'd never let someone like my mother herd him anywhere.

"Next Saturday."

"Worry about the dress tomorrow. Time for that orgasm, kitten. Call me back on video chat because I'm watching this time."

———

WEST

. . .

"KITTEN, don't you have a witness to cross examine?"

Her call this morning was a surprise. She'd initiated a text before, but never a phone call. I was astride Astro, my favorite horse. I'd been out since sunrise checking the fence line. It was an odd place to talk, but I liked hearing her voice. It made me think she was here with me, riding beside me once more. That I could drag her into the stable again and fuck her like I had that day.

Fuck. I shifted in my saddle because I was getting a semi at the thought.

"Close," she replied. "The judge postponed the case because a juror got food poisoning. I actually have five minutes."

I couldn't help but smile and feel special. I tipped my hat back and loosened my hold on the reins. The sun was warm already. It was going to be a hot day. "And you gave that time to me?"

"It's five minutes where I'm going to cross examine *you*."

"About what?"

"Your father. You diverted last night. Again."

I frowned and was no longer hard. Instead of seeing Rory's come face in my mind, I saw Tank Million.

"Haven't we talked about him enough?"

"You're being a difficult witness."

"Rory," I said on a sigh.

"Tell me," she pushed.

"I told you yesterday."

"You told me he wanted money and that he hasn't come back yet."

"That's right. He hasn't. I haven't left anything out."

"Are you going to pay him?"

"I'm not giving him six figures a year for the rest of his life to stay away from us," I snapped.

"That's a lot of money."

Astro dipped his head to reach the grass and I released his reins entirely to let him graze.

"It is," I confirmed. I was on a rise, my house and stables in the distance. The tall grass waved in a slight breeze. It had been a wet summer so a soft green carpet spread out before me. I couldn't imagine being in one of the thousands of skyscrapers in New York right now. The crowds. The noise.

"I can sue him," she said.

"For what?"

"Blackmail."

I picked at a stain on my jeans. "I'm not sure how the law works in the state of New York, but I'm pretty sure blackmail isn't solved that way."

"I can shoot him."

I laughed at her feistiness. "You sure can, kitten."

"Have him arrested. Jed can work on that, can't he?"

"Are you protecting me?" I wondered.

"I... I don't like someone messing with you," she admitted.

I rubbed my chest again, somehow feeling... touched. The tiny, fierce woman wanted to watch out for me. To solve my problems. She didn't realize that wasn't how it worked. I did the protecting where a woman was concerned. With Tank Million, I took care of myself the only way that consistently worked. I steered clear of him and his shit. I'd deal with it only when I had to, sic Jed on him as Rory suggested, then return to my ranch. To my quiet life.

"The feeling's mutual," I said, suddenly bothered that I wasn't there to protect her because I knew shit was brewing with her job. "How's it going on the partner front?" I asked, done with talking about Tank.

She was getting the shaft. I knew it. Probably subconsciously she knew it as well, but me telling her that would only get her feathers ruffled. We weren't arguing or hate fucking like we seemed to be really good at, so that was a plus. Wait. A hate fuck would be better than no fuck where Rory was concerned and I loved it when she gave me that narrowed look all the while clenching that tight pussy around my dick. Shit, now I was hard.

"I'm the lawyer here. I ask the questions," she countered. Fuck, back to Tank.

I ran a hand over the back of my neck, felt the layer of sweat that I needed to shower off.

"I don't like people coming after me for money. As if that's all I am to them."

"That's happened a lot, I'm sure," she replied.

"More than you know."

"Women, I'm guessing."

"Yes." I wasn't going to tell her about Carrie. Rory hadn't asked about one specifically, and like a good witness, I only had to respond to direct questions. Besides, no woman wanted to know about a guy's past relationships. I sure as fuck didn't want to hear about the men Rory had been with.

"You don't like to be screwed over," she guessed.

"Do you?" I asked, hoping she'd catch on to what I was really asking her.

"So you'll ride the range, birth calves, bale hay, fix a well and whatever else you do and leave him be?"

"You've done your research. I do, in fact, do all those things. So yes. I'll leave him be. I have for twenty-nine years and it's suited me just fine."

"But he's your father."

I sighed. "Kitten, out of anyone I know, I'd think you'd understand that just because someone's your daddy doesn't mean they deserve that title."

Yeah, that shut her right up.

 ORY

I WAS THINKING of West as I went around the corner. I was headed out to find a dress for the gala. I ran into someone and startled. Instinctively, I said, "Sorry," and I raised my hand. As soon as it made contact with a hard chest, I stepped back. "Jesus, Mike. What are you doing?"

I hated apologizing. I did it all the time, probably because women were subconsciously trained to do so. Like now. *I* shouldn't have been sorry. He should have because he'd been standing in the way.

Except he would never even think of it.

He smiled and I frowned. Yeah, I'd gone out for drinks with this guy. Considered him handsome. Smart. Maybe even sexy, although I inwardly cringed that I'd spent a second on that. Because in comparison to West, he was a smarmy little ass.

"I know about you and how you got the Wainright deal," he said, not looking me in the eye but tugging on a cufflink.

I stepped to go around him, but he pushed off the wall, blocking me.

"North's a hard negotiator, but both sides are happy."

He grimaced. "That cowgirl? I'm talking about West."

An instant rush of adrenaline flooded my blood. I felt as if I was driving and had to slam on the brakes to avoid something in the road. "The patent holder."

"Yeah, him." A sly smile spread across his face as he leaned in. "I have to hand it to you. Fucking someone on the other side of the deal isn't something I expected from you." He took his time sliding his gaze down my body. "You do have what it takes."

"You're being ridiculous," I countered.

"Am I? Why else would you be invited to Billion-aire Ranch?"

Huh. He'd done *some* work on the project.

"Jealousy doesn't look good on you," I countered.

"Me? Jealous of fucking a hick from the sticks? Does he even talk?" He paused, narrowed his eyes. "Hmm. Maybe it was better that way."

"You're disgusting." And an idiot. West might live in the middle of absolutely nowhere, but he had to be the smartest person I knew. Matthew was brilliant. My father was cunning. But West? He'd gone to MIT but hadn't dropped out because he couldn't hack it. He was probably too intelligent since his inventions were revolutionary.

As for the middle of nowhere? West's ranch was looking pretty damned spectacular right about now. A place where there were no Mikes or other assholes sounded pretty perfect.

He shrugged, then adjusted his gray tie—probably chosen to match my dad's. "I'm not the one who fucked for a promotion."

I had no idea how he'd figured it out. West wasn't going to blab, especially to Mike who he considered a dumbass. North didn't know either. I'd left the office after the meeting with North, not West. He hadn't even been in the helicopter. "You're way off with this. I was with North Wainright, not her brother. As you saw at the meeting, he wasn't too interested in contract work."

"Reasonable doubt."

I frowned, crossed my arms over my chest. "What?"

"A jury only needs to be swayed by reasonable doubt, not actual proof or evidence."

Meaning Mike could talk his way into my father and the other partners thinking it was *possible* the deed had happened instead of didn't. I'd left with North. North was West's sister. West had a penis. I had a vagina. We'd been in the same state at the same time.

I stepped back. I didn't have to stand here and listen to him. "Fuck off, Mike."

He tipped his head back and laughed. "Oh, daddy's perfect little girl swears. I can see I've struck a nerve. Don't worry, I'll keep your secret."

His laughter had people nearby looking our way. Clearly someone being amused was a surprise around here.

Daddy's little girl? As if. He knew as well as I that I'd been given zero perks for being the daughter of a founding partner. I had to work harder. Prove myself more. In Mike's eyes, even fuck a client. If I'd been given any kind of advantage, I'd have been partner years ago. Except I still hadn't gotten it, even after being promised the promotion after closing the Wain-right deal.

"But now that I know how low you're willing to go —probably all the way to your knees—I'm not playing nice. That partner spot is mine."

He looked me over again, then walked off.

I stood there, mortified. Shaking. Panicked.

A phone rang behind me. Voices carried from desks across the floor. The scent of coffee lingered from the break room. I hastily made my way to the bathroom and locked myself in the corner stall. I set a hand on the cool metal, stared at a little dent. I took a breath, let it out. Then another. Thankfully, no others were occupied and I had a moment to collect myself. No one was going to bother me. No one sticking their head in the stall wanting me for something. I was free from my father or Mike or any other man in the building.

I wanted to call West. To talk to him. To have him call me *good girl* and tell me everything was going to be okay.

There was no crying to West over this. Not because we *had* slept together, but because I knew what he'd say. That the job wasn't worth what I was putting myself through. That I worked *all* the time. I had no life, only a few friends, but didn't go have fun with them. I didn't take vacations. Spa days. I didn't even *like* my family.

I didn't like much of anything. Had it always been this way or had a few days in Montana given me a peek at my reality. The reality I chose intentionally. And for what?

I was fighting for a role that wasn't going to be earned by merit alone. If Mike thought I'd slept with West to get the corner office, what did others in the office think about me? Would they think I'd *earned* the partnership? Did they respect me? Did they see me as a lawyer skilled enough to be partner or for some other false reason? Did my father even see me as talented or solely as another lawyer to overwork for a stockpile of billable hours?

Would I ever really know?

Did I even want this any longer? I couldn't believe I was even considering it, but West was possibly right. Was the partnership worth it? I'd thought it was the ultimate goal. Ever since I was a kid, I wanted to work beside my dad. To have the Sullivan name in the business title mean more than just him. I'd worked for it. Taking advanced classes and getting all A's in high school. Excelling at Columbia. Pushing it through law school and interning here every free minute I had. I'd been free labor to my father for those years. Then once I passed the Bar, the clock on my billable meter had started and hadn't shut off since. Associates were billed at five hundred dollars an hour. I sure as shit didn't make that. Was I nothing more than a really good return on investment to my father?

I imagined myself in that office two floors up. Would I feel any different? Would my father see me differently? An equal? A daughter to be proud of? Would my mother still push me to quit if I was partner so I could base my happiness on something so trivial as a dress to a charity gala?

I rubbed my temple, wondering what I would even do with myself if I didn't walk through the doors of Nixon, Sullivan and Proctor seven days a week. I huffed out a laugh remembering that West had said North would hire me. She was a savvy business-woman. Her legal team that had been on our deal had consisted almost entirely of women. It was a billion-dollar corporation. All items I considered pros, not cons.

Except it was in Montana. Montana!

Someone came into the bathroom and washed her hands, reminding me I couldn't linger here forever. I had a stupid dress to buy and work to do I no longer liked.

Why had I never hated my life before now? God, Montana couldn't be any worse than this and that alone scared the shit out of me.

———

WEST

IT'S SIX AM HERE. I picture you sitting at your desk in one of those sexy as fuck dresses prepping for a case where you rip the opposing counsel's balls off. Here's a pic of my morning.

I snapped a picture of the sun coming up, the pink hint in the east growing brighter. The color of the grass was shifting from black to intense green. Fuck, it was beautiful. Yet I'd never felt more alone standing out here.

I attached the image and hit send, then went to the stables to start my chores. An hour later, dusty and sweaty, I checked my cell. Fuck, I was turning into Rory attached to her phone.

No response.

Kitten.

I didn't send any more texts after that, but I spent

my day worrying about why she wasn't replying. It'd been over a week since I dropped her at the airport like the asshole my siblings said I was. I hadn't wanted her involved with the fuckery surrounding Tank. I also hadn't wanted her to be more than the fling we'd originally agreed on. So getting rid of her so I could focus on Tank had been how I'd done it. Ended it with her, neat and tidy, just like she'd wanted.

Except we'd talked and messaged every day since. It wasn't over. I was kidding myself otherwise. I didn't know what it was, but I wanted to talk to her more than anyone else. I thought about her way more than I should.

I didn't need her as a complication though. Carrie had proved that with how she'd used me. And Carrie had been just like Rory was. Driven. Focused. A city girl with no intention or ability to survive in Big Sky country.

Even though she wanted the corner office, Rory wasn't anything like Carrie.

By the time I'd finished my dinner and hadn't heard from her, I drove to the big house. Why? I needed to understand a woman, which I sure as hell wasn't going to figure out on my own. I could ask East or South because they'd found the loves of their lives, but I had a feeling they'd just tell me the man basics. To say sorry to your woman for things you didn't even know you did and to fuck her into happiness.

That wasn't going to work with Rory because I hadn't done anything—that I knew of—and there was no way I could fuck her long distance even though we'd done a pretty good job of making do with phones and video chat.

I went in the back door. Eddie, North's dog, greeted me. I gave him some good pets then grabbed a bone from the bowl on the kitchen counter. Turning, I held up the treat. Eddie licked his lips and plopped his butt down on the hardwood, gaze laser focused.

I tossed it in the air and he caught it with expert precision. "Good boy." I pet him again.

"I think he likes you better," North said, coming into the kitchen.

She'd changed from the office attire into shorts and a MSU t-shirt. No shoes.

"Of course he does," I replied, although my words were proved wrong when Eddie went over to North, tail furiously wagging.

"You missed dinner," she said, making goofy faces at the dog. "Fajitas. Leftovers are in the fridge."

I held up my hand. "I already ate. I need a woman's take."

She looked up from Eddie and her face brightened. "Oooh, you've got girl trouble."

I dropped onto one of the stools at the center island.

"I'm worried about Rory. She's not returning my texts."

A pale brow arched. "You're texting? Like high schoolers? I wonder if she'll let you touch her boob beneath the bleachers." I glared and she sighed. "Wow, okay."

"We've been chatting since she left." I left out the phone and video sex. "Today it's radio silence."

"She's a busy woman."

I ran a hand over my face. "I know that. I tried to get her to wind the shit down, but it doesn't stick."

"Meaning post-orgasmic bliss only lasts so long."

I gave her a pointed look. "You want to talk about my sex life? Really?"

She frowned. "Yeah, no."

"Her dad hasn't given her the promised partnership," I explained. "Her mother sounds like a high-society flake and from what I gather, her brother is a tough act to follow."

"None of that is new though," she considered, leaning forward and resting her forearms on the granite. "What's changed to make her upset about it now?"

Her blue eyes met mine and then she smiled. "Oh. You."

I felt uncomfortable from her words. While I wanted to believe I made Rory think twice about her insane and what-I-pictured-as-miserable life, I didn't have that much influence. I didn't want it.

I told North that.

"It makes you responsible for someone," she replied, then cocked her head. "You look like you think that's a problem."

"It is. Jesus." I paused, tried to figure out how I was feeling. "Her being around me has made her unhappy." That was the last thing I wanted to do. I'd satisfied her body but fucked up her mind.

Maybe the feeling was mutual because I was talking to my *sister* about girls.

The look she gave me was full of pity. Or concern. "That's what you think? That this is your fault?"

I stood, paced. "Isn't it? I mean, she was perfectly happy being a wound tight lawyer before she met me."

"No, she was a perfectly miserable, wound tight lawyer who didn't *know* she was unhappy. She was that way long before she came to Montana. All you did was show her something better."

"Better?"

She came around the island and set her hand on

my arm. Eddie followed and nuzzled my leg for attention. "You sell yourself so short, West. You're good for her. You could be good for each other. Why do you think I set this all up?"

I didn't understand the ache in my chest. Didn't like it. I was feeling things and I wasn't used to it. It was uncomfortable and confusing.

"It's all about you, isn't it?" I asked.

She pursed her lips and reminded me of scolding schoolteacher. "You can't turn this on me. You came here specifically for my advice and I'm giving it to you."

"You haven't given me advice at all," I countered.

"Fine, here's the advice. Get out of your house and go live."

I frowned down at North. "What the fuck are you talking about? I'm outside all the time."

She stepped away, sighed. "For a guy as smart as you, you're an idiot. You might not work eighty hours a week, but you don't have a life. Go live it, and I think it's possible it could be with Rory."

"She's in New York!" I said, a little louder than I wanted.

Her eyes widened in obvious surprise. East was the hotheaded one, not me. "So? It might be all concrete but millions of people like it there."

My cell rang from my back pocket. I pulled it out, read the display. *Rory.*

"It's her." I turned and went out onto the back patio, leaving North behind. "Kitten," I said when I answered.

"Hi," she replied, her voice soft.

"What's the matter?" I asked. I didn't know what it was, but I was going to fix it. I felt determined to take care of whatever the hell was bothering her.

"I'm tired. Long day."

"That's not new," I replied. "What's wrong?"

"Why are you being nice?"

I frowned as I looked out over the Wainright land. "What do you mean, why am I being nice? I'm not an asshole."

"Why do you care?" she added.

"Do you *want* me to be a dick to you and not give a shit?"

"Look, West. I don't know what we're doing here."

"We're not doing anything," I replied.

"Exactly. So why are we even talking? I mean, the deal's done. I'm not returning to Montana. It's not like we're going to have sex again."

"We decided that early on, didn't we?"

"Yes."

I agreed with her. The words were all right. But the feelings were off.

"Why call me then? Why not just text me and say goodbye?"

She was silent for a minute, which was telling.

"What's going on, kitten?"

"Why do you always push?"

"Why do you always fight when you're afraid?" I countered. "Is it the dress?"

"God, out of all the people I didn't think you'd be one to think my life revolves around a stupid dress."

"You know I like you better *out* of your dresses. What's going on at work?"

"Why do you think I'm upset about work?"

"Because you're upset about something and work's all you do."

"Because I'm a woman?" she snapped.

"All right, kitten. If you were here, that sass would get your ass spanked. Since you're not, I need you tell me what the fuck is going on. Others might fall for your tough act, but you don't fool me."

"Fuck you."

I grinned. I loved that sass. I just wished she was here so I could shut that shit off. Some rope would work. So would my cock down her throat. "Kitten, I told you. *I* do the fucking."

She hung up.

I pulled the cell from my ear and stared at it. Shaking my head, I ran my hand over my face. "Fuck," I breathed.

The cell rang and I answered it. Didn't say anything.

I knew Rory was there, but she was quiet. Her mind was so fucking busy I wasn't sure how she kept all those flaming balls of shit that was her job in the air.

"I... I just want to know if you like me because I'm going to be partner or..." She took a deep breath. "Or because I'm me."

My heart ached for her. Yeah, my fucking heart. I wanted to reach out and grab her and pull her into a hug, to kiss the top of her head and make all this shit she's dealing with just go away.

"You already know the answer to that," I said, my voice low. Calm. "Kitten, you forget I like you best stripped bare. No work. No phones or laptops. No family. No idiot coworkers. Just you giving yourself to me."

"I think... I think you're the only one who's seen the real me."

"I like what I see, kitten. The question is, do you?"

This time, when she hung up, I knew she wasn't calling back.

I went back inside. North was pulling an ice cream sandwich out of the freezer. "Everything okay?"

I shrugged. "Not sure."

"You want to help her," she said, opening the wrapper.

"I live here. She's not coming back."

"Go to New York. Be there for her."

"You mean the gala," I murmured.

"What gala?"

"There's some charity event on Saturday night. Her mother's in charge of it or on some committee. I guess her brother's got a fiancée, there's a table they bought and some fucker named Mark she's supposed to marry and make babies with is going to be there."

Her eyebrows went up. "Do you want her to marry and make babies with a guy named Mark?"

I glared. "He probably wears pink pants with lobsters embroidered on them."

Her lips twitched.

"Probably couldn't find a clit without a headlamp and an online video tutorial," I added. Rory's pleasure was mine, not some New York dumbass.

North couldn't hold back the laugh. "Go to the gala."

"You're not serious."

"Be her date," she said, ignoring me. "There's nothing worse than going solo to a fancy event like that, especially if her mother's making plans for her and it's bothering her this much."

"*Be her date*?" I asked, as if she was asking me to have my teeth pulled to make room for a bit.

"It's a concept to you, I know," she replied, the words heavily laced with sarcasm.

"And to you," I countered.

She shrugged. "If you want Rory, you're going to have to do it. Be there for her. It's what she wants."

I frowned. "How the hell do you know that?"

She shrugged. "Because a woman like her isn't going to *ever* ask for help, especially from someone who is anti-city, anti-party, anti-people." She gave me a pointed look. Yeah, she had me pegged. "Rory's too self-reliant, especially with what you're telling me about her family. But she wants *you,* West, otherwise I promise she wouldn't be calling."

"Why do you say that?" I asked, which might show how dumb I was.

"Like you said, you both wanted no strings. A fling. If that was what she wanted, she would've left you in her plane's dust."

She took a bite of her ice cream sandwich and walked off, Eddie following.

Did she want me to go to the gala? Did she want me in general?

I had no fucking clue.

All I knew was that I didn't want this Mark character anywhere near her. If she wanted to make babies, she could do it with me. No. No! No fucking babies. Practice. We could practice.

 EST

"WHAT?" I snapped, dropping the ends of the bow tie to answer the call.

"What crawled up your ass?" East asked.

"Nothing. Just remembering why I like being a rancher."

I dropped into the plush couch of the Wainright jet, let my head fall back against the cushion.

"Yeah, well, it's good you're already cranky because what I've got to share isn't going to help."

"What?" I asked again.

"Tank went to the media."

I sat up. "What does he say?"

"Look for yourself."

"I'm somewhere over Ohio right now."

"Over... you're—why?"

"I'm going to New York. I'm on the jet."

"Holy shit. You're going for the lawyer?"

"Rory," I said, reminding him of her name. "I'm going to a gala. For Rory."

"A gala. I didn't even know you knew that word."

"Never thought I'd be going to one," I sighed, tugging at the snug collar of my dress shirt.

Once I decided to take North's advice and support Rory at the event, she helped me with getting a rush job on a tuxedo. I couldn't go into a store and buy one off the rack, even if they did sell them in Montana. Which they didn't. She helped get the suit, but wasn't here to help me with putting it on. I was good with all of it, but the bow tie probably wasn't going to happen.

"Then check out the articles on your phone."

"Give me the highlights."

"Macon's gay, so who's the daddy?"

I rubbed my temple. "Fuck. Are North and South okay?"

"They're both pissed, but it doesn't change anything. From the article and from our chat with

Tank, he only knows he made us and that's based solely on you looking alike."

"I assume North is going to handle PR and damage control?"

"Jed said on Monday. He's shut down the house's internet until then."

Smart guy. If anything came up over the weekend, I was sure a PR person would reach out to him. Until then, we didn't need to rush on anything.

"Good. I'll be back by then."

"You're not going to stay?"

I shook my head, but he couldn't see. "This isn't a relationship, East. It's... nothing. She's got work. That's *all* she's got."

"So if she wants to have you as well, she's got to give up her job?"

"A job doesn't keep her warm at night," I replied. "The only reason I'm going is because she outright told me this wasn't a thing. That she was getting the corner office, not a relationship."

"And you don't do them because of that Carrie woman back in college who chose a career over you."

"She *used* me for that career. Then she dropped me."

"You think Rory's using you for her career?"

"No. She used me for sex and that's fine by me."

"So you're there for sex."

"I won't turn it down." Hell, no. I was going to the gala then going to get inside Rory. If the event was as miserable as I imagined, then she'd need to get out of her head after. Doing that meant spanking her ass a nice hot pink before fucking her long and hard.

East sighed. "Whatever. Call me when you're home."

He hung up and I flopped back on the couch again, pulling up the first article on my phone.

Why did everyone want something from me, then when they didn't get it, they fucked me over? Sure, Tank affected the others, but I *looked like him.* The articles laid it all out. I was his look alike, so I'd be dealing with the fallout.

It only went to prove that it wasn't worth trusting anyone. It was only a matter of time before being used.

What made Rory perfect was that she was only using me for my dick. And I liked the simplicity in that.

Right?

———

RORY

. . .

THE GALA WAS in full swing. Four hundred guests filled the banquet hall at the posh hotel. The view was of the Hudson and New Jersey beyond. A band was playing, the drinks were flowing and waiters were diligent in passing out a variety of hors d'oeuvres. I was standing with my mother and Hadley eyeing the engagement ring on her left hand. I had to give my brother credit, it was gorgeous. And huge. No one within twenty feet could miss seeing the huge center diamond with smaller ones encircling it.

They were gushing over the thing. I was on my second glass of champagne. I liked Hadley. She was... sweet. But vain.

"I liked the one with the emerald," she began,

"Too flashy," my mother replied, then looked over my dress, which she'd said was *too flashy* for a charity event the second she saw me in it.

I rolled my eyes at her dig. I wore a fifties-style dress, something classic Grace Kelly would have worn in *Rear Window*. Cap sleeves, slim through the bodice and a flared skirt. It was the low square neckline in the front that made it modern, offering a hint of cleavage. It was the back that I'd fallen in love with. Instead of continuing the black silk, it had a panel of matching lace, all the way to the waist. I'd seen it and fallen in love.

My mother had seen it and pursed her lips in disapproval.

"You'll have to tell me what you think of the caterer," Mother said to Hadley. "They are doing the event over Labor Day weekend and I want to give them all the feedback they need to make that one a success." Hadley had already been pulled into society events, filling the space my mother hoped I'd take.

I saw no flaws with the food, which meant the caterer was doing a great job.

"Did you coordinate your nail appointment with mine for Tuesday?" she asked Hadley next. "Everyone will not believe the ring."

"Yes. For eleven," she replied with a nod. Her blonde hair was sleek and pulled back into a low bun at the nape of her neck.

"Then we'll lunch afterwards," Mother said.

She got the daughter she'd always wanted in Hadley. I didn't do manicures or lunches with my mother—except for a rare scheduled one—because I worked.

Matthew came over, set his hand on Hadley's bare shoulder. She wore a pale blue strapless dress, which matched my brother's pocket square. He was in a tuxedo and as a couple, they looked sharp. The perfect rich New York pair.

"Rory, Father is looking for you." He held a glass of seltzer. No alcohol for him in case he needed to return to the hospital. My mother had told me he wasn't on call—he wouldn't be here otherwise—but he lived to operate so there was no way he'd let a glass of whiskey make him miss the chance.

I scanned the crowd. Dinner hadn't been served yet. It was only the cocktail hour so I homed in on the bars scattered around the ballroom.

I found him and turned to go.

"When you're done come back as Mark Rutherford is around here somewhere," Mother said. "He's sitting at our table."

"I told you I wasn't interested," I replied. Frustrated. I thought of West. He was the guy I'd want to sit with. If he weren't a rancher. In Montana.

I had no idea what we'd been doing over the past two weeks since I'd flown home. Calling. Texting. Video *sexting*. I liked being with him two time zones apart more than any other guy I'd dated face to face.

He'd proven he wasn't a player, but he wanted different things. Different *places*.

I'd hung up on him the other day, realizing I'd been too vulnerable. I'd shared too much. We hadn't talked since.

She waved her hand. "He's interested in seeing

you." A sly wink followed that which only made her look like she had something in her eye.

"It's not fair to Mark, Mother." There was no way he could ever compare to West. "If he's trying to meet someone, he should be matched with a woman who's interested. I'm not," I said again.

"He's partner in his own law firm. Why do you have to keep pushing? He can take care of you."

I glanced at Hadley, who smiled. She was a total Stepford wife-in-training and she probably only saw me as being difficult, not ambitious.

"I can take care of myself."

I didn't linger any longer, just cut through the crowd to join my father.

"Ah, there you are." He looked good in his crisp tuxedo. He had a drink in hand and his cronies around him. "You remember the others."

I smiled and nodded. "Of course."

Of the four men, one was a judge, the other a hedge fund manager, another was a pilot if I remembered correctly and the last was a lawyer who ran his own firm.

"Rory's our newest partner."

If thoughts could screech like car tires, mine sure did.

"What?" I asked, staring wide eyed at my father.

He grinned. "Congratulations, Rory."

I glanced at the other men who were smiling as well. This wasn't a joke.

"Oh my God. Wow. This is..."

Everything.

I shook the other men's hands and my dad set his on my shoulder.

"She's here with Mark Rutherford. Of your firm, Charles."

"A two-partner relationship. Impressive." Charles replied, seemingly pleased with his employee.

"I'm not here with Mark," I clarified. I felt like I was floating on a cloud, but I still had to make sure my mother didn't have me engaged by the end of the night. I'd met Mark, in passing, a time or two. I was sure he was a decent guy and I wanted to save him from whatever my mother had brewing. "I'm seeing someone."

I had no idea why that popped out. Maybe my brain had turned to mush because... oh my God! I was partner!

"Oh?" My father asked, chest puffing up. Yeah, now he was interested in me. "Who?"

Who? "A man I met in Montana."

Dad frowned. "Montana? When you were there for work?"

"Yes."

"Does he work for Wainright Holdings?"

I shook my head. West didn't work for Wainright Holdings. I just wasn't going to explain that he was a Wainright. "He's a rancher."

Dad's face crinkled as if he could smell the cow manure from here. The other men glanced at each other as if I were a child who'd gone off to college and returned home goth.

"Why the hell would you want to get involved with a man like that? You're partner now, not a cowgirl."

I did have the boots though.

If he'd asked, I could have told him West was a billionaire, a *Wainright*. Then all he'd want him for was his money.

"The Montana thing was a fling," he told me. "Mark is more fitting."

I was frustrated. My happiness was being tainted by my father's judgment about West. But also because I had a quick sense that I would be expected to find the right man to go with the corner office. Not just any man, but one my parents thought was appropriate. And definitely not a rancher. He was devaluing my choices, my opinions, forcing me to follow his.

I'd called West *just a rancher* myself, and to his face, but had learned that he was so much more.

Smart, sexy... kind.

The band stopped playing, indication that dinner was being served. He gave his friends a simple chin lift of farewell and took my elbow.

A waiter came up and I moved closer to my father for him to pass.

"Mark is also here, not in some podunk state. You can sit beside him at the meal and decide."

Decide? It didn't sound like he was giving me a choice.

"I'm *not interested* in Mark," I said for the millionth time.

"Don't let your mother hear you're interested in a dusty, hick Montana rancher," he added.

"Why's that?"

I froze and Dad's hand came off my arm. I recognized that voice. Deep, calm. Even.

Turning, I knew who I'd see, but I was still stunned.

"West," I whispered. He was here!

West, in his bespoke tuxedo, moved close and wrapped his arm about my waist. He kissed my temple in a way that... fuck, it was perfect. For the first time tonight, I felt safe. As if I wasn't alone. No, not just tonight. All week. Ever since I got on that plane in Bozeman. *He* was the person I wanted to tell about the promotion. *He* was the one who'd consistently asked because he knew it was my dream.

"Kitten, you look incredible," he whispered right by my ear. His warm breath fanned my skin.

"I... I got the partnership."

His eyes widened, then he smiled. "Good girl, kitten. I'm proud of you."

I stared at him. He stared at me. I felt sheer happiness. Because of the promotion, but also because of West's praise. And the fact that he was here for me.

"Who the hell are you?" Dad asked.

I had to look away. Dad was eyeing how West kept me by his side, then studied him from head to toe. West's hair was cut and groomed. Every bit of his tuxedo fit him perfectly. Because he was so big, it had to have been custom made. He sure as hell didn't look like a rancher. He looked... like a billionaire. And gorgeous.

Every woman in the room was eyeing him.

"I'm the hick Montana rancher."

The band started up with soft background music for the meal.

Dad didn't say anything, just took a swig of his drink. Yeah, West wasn't in dusty wranglers and chaps. No Stetson or snap shirt. No lasso or big belt buckle. Nothing like my father imagined him to be. *Nothing* like I'd imagined either. He sure cleaned up well. Different, not better.

"Rory just mentioned she was seeing someone from Montana," my father commented.

West glanced down at me. Even with my heels, he was still so much taller. "Really? We do see a lot of each other, don't we, kitten?"

The corners of his eyes crinkled with amusement as I felt my cheeks heat.

"I just didn't expect—"

West looked up at my father's words and gave my side a gentle squeeze. "Someone less dusty? You must be Rory's father. I've heard about you."

"And I only heard of you now."

"West Wainright."

It took Dad a second, but he figured out who West was, and not just a hick. When he did, his whole demeanor changed.

"Good to meet you." Dad held out his hand and West shook it. "Ian Sullivan. Your family has an impressive business."

"That's what happens when a woman runs the company," West replied.

Most people were in their seats eating the salad course. Waiters were passing out the remaining plates now. Some lingered like we did, talking.

I glanced toward our table. My mother was staring at West with a gleam in her eye. West made Mark Rutherford look like a wet-behind-the-ears college kid. West was *all* man... and he had his hand around *my* waist. My mother was probably planning wedding floral arrangements right now.

Holy hell, he'd come all the way to New York for me.

"You'll sit with us at dinner, won't you?" Dad asked.

Now he was interested in a Montana rancher. Nine zeros had a way of changing his perspective.

I looked up at West when I asked, "I'm going to use the ladies' room before we eat."

He turned his attention to me, those dark eyes assessing.

"You'll be okay on your own?" I asked.

Being worried about a big brawny guy like him was probably laughable, but this wasn't his thing. These people were ruthless and he'd just learned that about my dad. About how the only reason he'd shaken West's hand was because he was a billionaire. I wanted to... protect him.

"I'll be fine, kitten."

Yeah, he sure was.

———

WEST

I watched Rory walk away, took in the sway of her hips and that fucking-hot lace that covered her back. She wasn't wearing a bra. I knew it and so did every man in the room.

I was possessive of this woman, especially here, on her turf. In this huge fucking city where I couldn't hide her away.

"Drink?" Ian asked.

I nodded and followed him to the bar. I saw a resemblance with Rory. They had the same eyes. The same dark hair.

"Congratulate your sister on a solid deal," he began, then gave his order to the bartender. I gave mine.

He leaned against the bar, looked me over again.

"I will," I replied.

"Rory wouldn't have fucked you if you weren't part of the deal."

I narrowed my eyes. What the fuck? I was stuck on the fact that this man—Rory's father—knew we had sex. Had she told him? Hell, no. Then who? And why? And why was he talking about his daughter's sex life?

"Why would you say that?" I asked neutrally.

"Because she's driven. That corner office was hers if the contract was signed."

"I heard about that and that the partnership is now hers."

"That's right. Because she put initiative into it. Did whatever it took to make it happen."

I was processing that when the little shit Mike Spain joined us.

Rory had been right. This gala was a shit show. I hadn't even met her mother or the Mark guy yet.

Rory's father took our drinks from the bartender and handed me my whiskey.

"Mike, you remember West Wainright, I assume."

Mike, in his tuxedo, didn't look any less like an asshole.

He nodded in greeting. "Yes, the patent holder."

Rory's father's eyes widened. "Ah, that explains everything, and the reason she got the promotion."

Mike's face went slack. "What? You made Rory partner? I told you she slept with him."

Mike had told Sullivan we'd fucked.

"Yes, and I reward dedication like that," Ian told him.

"She gets the job because she spread her legs? Are you serious?"

"Watch it," I snapped.

Mike was glaring at Ian, so I wasn't sure if his cheeks went ruddy and his jaw clenched because of my tone or because of what his boss did.

Rory's father didn't say a word. Didn't defend his daughter or put Mike in his place, preferably in the unemployment line. I took a sip of his drink as anger tightened my muscles. My fist clenched at my sides. I wasn't sure which guy to punch.

"How do you know any of this, Mike?" I asked through gritted teeth. My voice was low and calm. He didn't know me well, so he puffed up his chest, unaware that I was seconds away from ripping his head from his body.

"Reasonable doubt," he said, with a confident chin lift. "I can explain it to you, if need be."

He hadn't studied my CV or my education as well as Rory had. "I'm well aware of what's true versus what's perceived."

"Are you saying you didn't fuck her?"

Ian was watching and waiting for my answer. He wasn't shutting Mike up like a good father should. With his fist to the teeth. He wanted to know for himself. Which was fucking twisted.

My eyes narrowed. I took a step toward Mike and he retreated. Then I reached out and gripped his shoulder, tugged him close. Squeezed the shit out of him. I loomed and made sure he didn't miss what I had to say.

"I haven't said anything at all, but I sure as shit wouldn't be speaking about Rory the way you are. You're just as dumb as I thought. You tattled like a kindergartner and all it did was give Rory the job."

"The man's right," Ian added. Was he siding with me? What the actual fuck? "She got the job because she showed initiative. Did whatever it took to close the deal."

I couldn't stand here a second longer. I tossed back my drink, set the glass on the bar. I was here for Rory. Only her.

 EST

I FOUND RORY OUTSIDE THE LADIES' room chatting with another woman in a silver dress covered in sequins. She looked up as I approached and she was smiling.

Fuck. She was happy. From across the room, she was radiant. She'd made partner and she was thrilled. Because she thought she'd earned it.

And not on her back.

Except she'd gotten the position because her father was a... fuck, what was a man like him? Creep didn't do it. Asshole was only part of it. A man who awarded a woman for using sex as a business tactic? A creepy asshole. But when it was a father and daughter? Scum.

I couldn't tell her the chat I'd just had. No way. Her father wouldn't have given her the job if she wasn't smart and experienced lawyer. She'd worked at the company for years and I was sure her performance record was impeccable and she probably had more billable hours than any other associate, especially that little shit Mike.

She'd earned the promotion. But the idea of Ian and the others believed she'd... take one for the team didn't sit right. Hell, it made me feel sick.

I thought Tank Million was bad, but he was tame in comparison. He'd gone to the papers because he hadn't gotten his money. To try and hurt us out of spite or just... assholishness. Whatever. But Ian Sullivan? He and Macon would have gotten along really well.

The fuckers.

"Hi," she said. I took her hand in mine. After two weeks of talking, texting and video calls, being able to touch her was something I hadn't realized I'd craved.

Her skin was so damned soft. Silky. She was even smaller and feminine than I remembered.

"What?" she asked and I realized I was just staring.

"I want you all to myself." I leaned down, breathed in her scent, felt her soft hair against my cheek. I'd come here for her, but I wasn't sure if I could go back to the party. Not with what I knew now. "I need in you. Now."

She turned her head so our eyes met. We were so close, our mouths only inches apart.

"Yes," she whispered.

I stood to my full height, looked around. The sign for the coat room caught my eye and I tugged her in that direction. Thankfully, the door was unlocked. I held it open for her and she stepped inside as I flicked on the light switch.

Rows of coat racks filled the space, all empty because it was summer. The door closed behind me and I flipped the lock.

She was facing me, her cheeks flushed, her breathing coming in little pants, which only made her breasts pillow above the line of her dress.

"I can't believe I made partner," she said, her voice full of wonder and surprise.

It was on the tip of my tongue to tell her the truth, but it wasn't my place. I wasn't her man. I was the guy she'd fucked on a business trip and the man who she'd talked with on the phone. Nothing more. We'd made it clear we didn't want that.

It wasn't my place to burst her bubble. She wanted

the job. Who the hell knew what she'd endured before now.

Hell, maybe *she* knew about the whole thing.

"Mike must be jealous," I said, trying to see. Because if she'd actually done just that, fucked me for the job...

No. I couldn't believe that. Then I thought of Tank. Maybe I should. People were assholes.

"I haven't seen him. But yes, he's going to freak. But I don't care. He's a dick."

"Your father must have thought you wrote one hell of a contract."

She shrugged. "It was years in the making. God, finally!" She tossed up her hands and that tightness about her when I'd first seen her at the Billings airport was gone. "I earned that spot. Fuck, I worked so hard. Do you have any idea what I've put up with?"

"I've met Mike. I've got a pretty good idea," I replied.

"You've also met my father. Sorry about that."

She didn't know. She had no idea the good ole boys network wasn't including her. Or including her because of their misogynistic fuckery.

I looked her over again, the prim but sexy dress. Those ridiculous heels. "I'm proud of you, kitten. I didn't pull you in here to talk about Mike or your father. I want you to show me what's under that dress."

"Black lace."

My dick was instantly hard. I shook my head. "This isn't a phone call. Show me."

"I can't take this dress off."

"Lift it, kitten."

Her fingers hooked around the hem of the poofy bottom and lifted it. Slowly, like she knew seeing one inch of black stocking covered leg at a time didn't make pre-cum leak from my dick.

"Fuck, garters?"

She smiled now, but it was coy. She knew how I was affected by her.

The dress moved higher to expose her matching lace covered pussy.

I had to get my hands on her so I stepped close and cupped her.

She gasped and went up on her toes.

"Drenched. These panties are ruined. That all for me?"

Her dark eyes dilated and a flush bloomed on her cheeks, then crept lower.

"Yes."

"Good girl." Fuck, she was perfect. Except for the fact that her goal in life was the complete opposite of everything I could ever want or imagine. Living in this huge city, dealing constantly with asshole coworkers. A father who... No. I had my hand on her pussy and for right now, she was mine.

Without breaking contact, I walked us backward until she bumped the wall.

"Here. Now."

"Yes."

I ripped the dainty panties at one hip, then the other, putting the damp lace in my pocket.

"Hold the dress up."

The fabric bunched in her hands as she held it up to her waist.

"Fuck, you're beautiful. I get to see you like this."

"Only you."

I flicked a gaze up from her bare pussy to her eyes. "That's right, kitten."

My fingers found her again, this time without anything in the way. She was so wet. Hot. Silky soft. I plunged two fingers into her.

She arched her back. "West. Yes!"

I was being aggressive, but I needed it. From the way her inner walls were rippling around my fingers and her arousal was coating my palm, she needed it too.

"Hurry," she breathed, reaching for the front of my

tuxedo pants and deftly opening them, pushing them along with my boxers down enough for my dick to spring free. She licked her lips as she eyed it.

"You want your mouth filled, kitten?"

She reached out, swiped the bead of pre-cum from the slit and brought it to her lips.

"Fuck," I growled. "Can't mess up that pretty lipstick. While I want you to go back out there and look like you just sucked my balls dry, it's probably not a good idea."

I wasn't giving her father or Mike or anyone anything to use against her. What we did together, no matter how dirty or wild, was between us. I'd never, *ever,* shame her like that, even if she didn't know it.

She squeezed the base and pumped me once. "Hurry then."

I pulled a condom from the interior pocket of my jacket and handed it to her. With deft—and eager—fingers, she ripped open the package and had us protected in seconds.

I wrapped an arm behind her and lifted her up, a hand cupping her ass. She wrapped her legs around my waist. Pushing at the layers of her dress, I shoved it out of the way, crushing it between our stomachs.

I lifted her a little higher and lined myself up at her entrance, then pulled her down as I thrust deep.

She groaned and pulsed around me. I was big and it had been two weeks. She clenched and milked and squeezed me.

"Fuck, keep doing that and I'm going to come."

She tried to move, but between my body and the wall, she was pinned. I pulled back, rammed home. "That what you need?"

"Yes."

I did it again. "Fucked by my big dick."

"Yes."

"Hard. Deep. You're going to go back out there and be sore. I'll give you what you need so you can go back to the life you've always wanted."

And I'd head back to Montana and clean up any fallout from Tank. Then go to the ranch and return to my quiet, peaceful life.

"Yes."

Sweat made my shirt cling. Her breaths had her tits practically bursting from the low neckline. Since I knew she wasn't wearing a bra, I tugged down the dress and her nipple popped free.

I wasn't a contortionist, too big to lean down and suck on it as I wanted. But seeing that pink tip, knowing how prim and proper she was in that dress and I could defile her like this...

Reaching between us with my free hand, I found her clit. "Time to come, kitten. Cream all over me."

She came first, always. It was my job to see to her pleasure and knew I could clear her mind and make her beg with my big dick and my calloused hands.

Her head went back and she clawed at my shoulders. I felt it even through my jacket.

"West," she moaned as she came, her clit swelling and pulsing under my thumb.

I felt a hot gush of her desire as she came.

I followed her, my balls emptying in heavy bursts filling the condom. Lost in her.

Her. Rory. I had no idea why this woman was perfect for me, that she was so dainty and proper, so prickly and sassy, yet let me defile her with my rough cowboy ways. I loved knowing I could make her like this, that no city slicker would be able to get her to drip down her thighs.

This pussy was mine. She was mine.

Except... she wasn't.

I pulled free and tossed the condom in a trashcan. I tucked myself back in my pants and watched as Rory smoothed down her dress.

"What do you see in that crowd?" I asked, thumbing over my shoulder indicating the ballroom.

"My life."

"You don't have to work for your father, you know."

She frowned. "I just made partner. It's what I've always wanted."

"At what expense, kitten? No life?"

"Work *is* my life."

I quirked my lips. "Yeah, I'm well aware of that."

"What's that supposed to mean?"

"It means you've been pushing yourself for this promotion ever since you were what... thirteen?"

"Ten."

I ran a hand over my face and smelled Rory's sweet pussy on my fingers. *Fuck.*

"For twenty years you've focused on this one thing."

"My brother's a neurosurgeon. I don't see you out there trying to convince him he got too much training," she countered.

"I didn't just fuck your brother. I was inside you. I see you when you let all those walls down. When you forget for five fucking minutes and see a different life."

"A life with you fucking me."

He shrugged. "I don't see you complaining."

I was so angry with her father that I wanted her as far away from that firm as possible. I hadn't seen the signs with North, but I knew every one with Rory. She needed out of that place. It was toxic for her. She just didn't know it.

"You can leave. Just walk out the door."

Her eyes widened. "Are you insane? And give up everything I've worked for? I got the job! I can't quit now."

"People who climb Everest don't stay at the top. They head back down and choose another adventure. It doesn't make them any less of an incredible climber."

"There's no air up there. They can't breathe. Jesus." She shook her head, as if I was being ridiculous.

I set my hands on her shoulders so she'd look at me. "Can you breathe? Have you stopped and taken a full breath? I bet the one and only time you did was when I kidnapped you."

Her mouth snapped shut.

"Yeah, that's what I thought. Kitten, you took a day for yourself because I forced you to do so. I gave you permission. I'm giving you permission to quit. To find something that makes you happy."

"I am happy!" she almost shouted.

"I just fucked you in a coat closet instead of eating a thousand-dollar-a-plate dinner with your family."

"We're a fling, West."

Yeah, sure.

"Right. You're hiding. You're hiding in a fucking coat closet."

"You pulled me in here," she countered. "Look, I'm not hiding."

"Not picking a life where you can be happy, hiding behind your job is *not* a life."

Her eyes narrowed. "You want to talk about hiding? Let's talk about you. You hide."

"Me?"

She circled her hands to knock mine away and began to pace the small room. "You. You leave MIT early because, why? Because you're too scared to keep going or too smart."

"A woman."

That stalled her, at least for a second. "A woman. So you walked away from the rest of college because things went bad with a woman."

"No, I did all that because she didn't love me. She loved my money and my last name."

"Right. So you went back to Montana and hid. You hide behind your sister."

I gave her a *what the fuck* look. "How the hell do I do that?"

She spun back around and stalked toward me. "You're the patent holder. You're the genius! You're the one who should be negotiating for what you created.

Put your own value on it. Yet you just give them to her to make the deals. You told me you don't care what happens with them. Because you're hiding. How long's it been since *you* were happy?"

About five minutes when I was balls deep inside of her.

She poked me in the chest. "Don't you dare mansplain my life to me, West Wainright. I'm happy. I've gotten what I wanted. I worked for it. Got it. Unlike you. Hiding on your ranch because you're afraid."

I sputtered because this was not how this was to go.

She lifted her chin. Smoothed her hand over her hair. "Thank you for coming, West. That orgasm was amazing. Go back to Montana. I'd drop you off at the airport, but I have a gala to get back to."

She turned and left, leaving me in the coat closet. She had everything she ever wanted, just like I'd expected all along. There were no surprises here, except for the fact that I wanted to go after her. To toss her over my shoulder again and walk off. Never to let her go.

But I didn't have to do that. She'd already done the walking away.

19

ORY

I STOOD in front of the floor to ceiling windows in my new office. Even only two floors up from where I'd worked for the past eight years, I could see so much more from this side of the building. The room was at least four times bigger than my tiny associate's space. I had two visitor chairs on the other side of my huge desk. Even a couch. A plant stood in the corner. A real plant, not a fake plastic one.

This morning, I'd been greeted by the floor's receptionist with a warm smile and a congratulations. Others had done the same, but didn't linger to chit chat, returning to their work. Franklin, another founding partner, had stuck his head in and congratulated me on doing so much for the firm. He'd smiled, then winked, before disappearing.

"Change of schedule," Jared said, coming into the room.

I glanced at him over my shoulder. He held the usual tablet and was staring at the screen. I could have been wearing Mickey Mouse ears and he probably wouldn't have noticed.

"Partner lunch meeting at noon. Not one. You have a dinner with the Simms client at seven, then a call with Hong Kong at nine-thirty. I shifted everything else around for the afternoon to adjust for lunch so check your online schedule."

"Thanks," I said. Fortunately, Jared was to remain my assistant. He knew me, knew my work habits. I couldn't imagine my day without his help.

"Heard the gala was a success," he said.

"It was."

It wasn't. Not at all. Okay, I'd gotten the promotion while there, but that was the highlight. Was it? Could it have been being in West's arms? Feeling him thrust deep inside me? Him talking dirty to me as I came all over him? Or was it when he called me his good girl?

No. It wasn't because we'd gotten in a fight. He'd

accused me of hiding. As if *he* wasn't the one who had his head buried in the proverbial sand. West avoided life more than anyone I knew. He was a genius, had a mind that could see things and puttered until it turned into something real. Something workable that changed an entire industry.

But he didn't care. It was *tinkering.*

One minute the orgasm had been so incredible I had almost screamed. The next, his dick was back in his pants and I'd left him in the coat closet, my torn panties in his pocket. I had no idea where he went, presumably back to Montana.

He didn't call. Didn't text. Didn't check in with me as he'd done the past two weeks. Whatever had been going on was now officially done.

Yeah, that had been a grand finale fuck.

"Congrats again on the promotion."

I smiled at him. "Thanks."

He nodded, then left.

It was a typical Monday morning. Nothing seemed to have changed except the location and size of my office. I had yet to see my improved paycheck but if I had lunch and dinner meetings, plus overseas phone calls late at night, I wasn't going to have any time to spend it.

There had been no party. No ticker tape parade. Not even a cake or cupcake or even a piece of candy.

My father had patted me on the shoulder, then told me I had to settle down with the right man. My mother had seen the partnership as another day at the office and all but pushed me into the chair beside Mark Rutherford. My brother and Hadley didn't even know about it because my father hadn't shared the news with the table. And if I had brought it up, it would have been considered self-aggrandizing.

This was my life. Right where I'd always wanted.

I wanted to lift my middle finger and mentally tell West to fuck off for even making me question it. Except...

This moment didn't feel like I'd expected. Sure, when my father told me I'd made partner, I'd been thrilled. He'd seemed proud even. But I'd thought it would be more special. That I'd have someone to share this with. My family, but they'd been like a dud firework. All expectation and no result.

It was only going to be me. Me and my bigger office and my billable hours. I had a fancier ladies' room and there wasn't just a coffee machine in the break room, but a coffee bar.

I felt... not happy. Not *unhappy* either. Like my life wasn't complete like I'd thought. West had been there the other night. Had congratulated me. Hugged me. Kissed my temple. Fucked the hell out of me. Called me kitten. His good girl.

But he was fleeting. Temporary. Because he thought this job was all consuming. That it was my life because I'd told him as much. Proven it by taking a phone call when he'd been eating me out. God, I'd been an idiot.

Ever since Saturday night, I'd been angry at him. Had slept horribly for two nights as I tossed and turned over our argument. Over what he'd insinuated about my life. While I'd known him for two weeks, which wasn't much, in that time we'd only been around each other for less than two days total.

He didn't know me! Know my wants and dreams.

No. He did. I'd told him what my dream was. This office. He hadn't stood in the way of it, hadn't kept me from it. I'd made it clear, *crystal clear*, my priorities.

The other night he'd said–mid-fuck–that he'd give me what I needed so I could get back to what I wanted.

That haunted me more than anything else. Because I'd *wanted* this job for so long I'd started to forget why. When I'd been a kid, it had been to be near my father. To have something in common with him. Then it was to keep up with Matthew. To make something of myself while being in his shadow. I couldn't be a doctor. No way. I'd always ride his coattails. But I could emulate my dad.

I was almost thirty. I didn't look up to my father in the same way now. My mother was driving me bonkers. God, even my father wanted me paired with Mark Rutherford, or some Mark Rutherford lookalike.

I didn't want Mark. If I was going to pick someone it would be... holy shit. It would be West. I'd enjoyed our calls and texts. Looked forward to them. Expected them... and him.

This job? I couldn't imagine anything else. But what if I didn't want it? That scared the shit out of me because it's all I ever wanted. Except now. I wasn't sure if I wanted it now. Was I like a spoiled child, begging for a toy and then when given it, they tossed it aside?

I needed some guidance and I knew just the person.

I dropped into my cushy leather chair and pulled up my contacts on my computer. I dialed the number before I thought twice. "Yes, hi. Rory Sullivan for North Wainright, please."

I knew her personal assistant. "Hi, Rory. Hold, please."

In less than a minute, North was on the line.

"Hi, Rory. I hope everything is okay."

It felt good that she asked that first thing, that she thought of me as a person, not a worker bee. Except I wasn't a drone any longer. I was the queen.

"Yes, thanks. There's no issue with the client, I assure you."

"Good. I received a call from Jared earlier saying that Michael Spain was now my contact at your firm."

From home, I'd worked all day yesterday to stop thinking about West. Jared had emailed to ensure I reached out to my clients and did hand-offs. A partner didn't have the same tasks as an associate, including working with the Wainrights on any contract follow up.

"Mike? Well, I'm sure he'll provide you with the best service."

She was quiet. "He's an asshole."

I couldn't help but laugh. "You're right, he is."

"Why is he taking over for you? I'm not thrilled having an asshole for my contact."

"I made partner."

"Oh. That's so great! Congratulations. I know that's been a dream of yours."

"Yes, it has," I agreed.

"I hear a but in there."

I sighed, bit my lip. I spun my chair around, faced

the impressive view again. "Can I ask you something? I mean, you became CEO last year."

"That's right."

"Did it... feel less than you expected?"

"My situation was different. Macon died and I inherited the position." She was quiet again. "Actually, we're more alike than I realized. You're in a family company as well. Our fathers ran, or in your case, *run* them."

I wasn't sure if West had told her that I knew Macon wasn't really her father. It didn't matter because he was the man who'd raised her. Groomed her.

"I started at Wainright Holdings in college."

"I interned here at the same time."

"Right. Well then. I guess I never answered your question. I wanted the job. God, did I. Partially because I hated Macon and a lot because I didn't like how he was running it. I'll just say he was far from ethical. I can do what I think is best for the company now, taking it in a new direction. Hopefully, forward. You have to keep working with your father. He'll still be your boss, right?"

"Yes."

"Around the same time last year, I met Jed. He made me see that there was more to life than work."

"Like shooting?" I kidded.

"That's right, Annie Oakley."

I couldn't help but smile. I liked North, liked the life she'd carved for herself. Doing the work she loved with the man she loved more beside her.

"I was free of Macon, free to make my life what I wanted, to make my work what I wanted. The entire company."

"I'm impressed by the number of women lawyers you have." I hadn't told her that before, not in a place to do so. Hopefully now I was.

"I bet you're the only female partner," she guessed.

"I am."

"I have a life now. Besides work."

"Jed."

"Yes. And my brothers. I've taken up knitting, but I'm terrible at it. Maisey just signed us up for a fall bowling league. God, I'm not sure if I can wear those rental shoes."

"I hope you've bought your own." I shuddered and she laughed.

"They don't have a heel!"

"My father's not going anywhere," I said. "If he retired or died–the first I doubt he'll ever do and the second will happen in his desk chair–I wouldn't take over the firm. There are two other founding partners and six others like me. That's not going to change." I rubbed my temple. "I think it's going to get worse. God, Mike's going to get the next partner spot, I'm sure."

"What do you want, Rory?" she asked, skipping a response about Mike. Thankfully.

"From you?"

"No. From yourself. From life."

"The corner office, this partnership," I replied immediately.

"Really? Let me guess. If you were like me, you work seven days a week. You're up at dawn and eat lunch at your desk. Your assistant gets you carry out for dinner before he leaves. Then you work until your eyes cross and you stumble home and into bed to sleep for five or six hours to do it all over again. It doesn't matter if you wear stilettos or a pant suit. You're never going to have a dick and you're always going to miss the real meetings which are at a line of urinals. I'd assume even off the books negotiations with judges occur in the same place."

"Um–"

"I'm sure there are women judges and other women in your office. They've either got a family and kids and will never advance out of their current position or they have no family waiting for them so they're expected to fill the void with a shit ton of billable hours."

"Mind read much?"

"I'm not a lawyer, but corporate life is corporate life. It's a man's world, at least in your office."

I dropped my head back against the chair. "God, it is. My father has never forgiven me for being born without a penis."

She didn't say anything.

"Oh my God," I whispered. "I've been trying to make up for that ever since."

"I'm sure West likes you a lot better without one," she replied.

I thought of West, of how the sex was amazing. I loved *his* dick.

"You're a good lawyer, Rory. I wouldn't have signed the contract otherwise. You're not stuck there, even if it feels like you are. You earned that partner position over years of work. You don't have to kill yourself to pay them back in gratitude."

"I know." Did I? I worked all day yesterday because it was what I did on Sunday. It was also because I felt I had to, because I had to ensure the other partners were assured they'd made the right decision. It had been a gorgeous day. I could have gone to Central

Park. A ball game. Walked through a museum. Anything.

I thought of what West said, that I'd climbed Everest getting the partnership. Could I breathe here at the top? Did I want to stay here? Did I *have* to? Could I climb down and start a new mountain?

For the first time, I felt like there were so many possibilities. That I could walk out that door and never see Mike Spain again. Never scrape for success or opportunity. Never listen to my father spout baseball analogies. My mother would be thrilled. Matthew wouldn't care.

"Any firm in New York would hire you. Or you could work for yourself." She laughed. "You can even come work for me."

"I accept."

"What?"

I popped to my feet and began to pace. Oh my God. Had I actually said that? I was excited and scared. Nervous and... crazy?

"Oh my God, North. I accept a legal position with your company."

"In Montana," she said, probably for confirmation.

"In Montana."

"Is there any other reason why you might want to

spontaneously relocate here? Like, my brother, for example?"

"There's nothing between us."

She laughed. And laughed. "Right. He just takes the corporate jet and goes to New York for any reason, let alone a woman. Ever."

"It's just–"

"Sex?"

I blushed and didn't want to reply.

"Fine, don't answer that."

"He made me see there's more to life than the one I have."

"Aw, isn't he sweet?"

It was my turn to laugh. "Don't let him hear you call him that. I don't know what we have. Okay? I feel things for him I've never felt for anyone else. I never considered possibilities with him because all I could see was being partner. But he's got his own issues."

"Yeah."

"He can't help me with mine and I can't help him with his."

"No, but you can be there for each other as you work on them," she replied. "That's what it's all about. Standing side by side."

"I've only gone it alone."

Because my family were so self-centered. My

parents expected things from me regardless of my own wants. My brother expected nothing. I was surrounded by family but it meant nothing.

I needed to make my own way. Find my own people.

Maybe. Just maybe—and crazily—it was in Montana.

Good thing I already had the cowgirl boots.

My father came to my door dressed in his usual black suit and silver tie. I hadn't seen or talked to him since the gala.

"My father's here. I have to go, but I haven't changed my mind. I want it," I said to North, setting the phone back in the cradle.

"This office looks good on you," he said, stepping in and looking around.

I blinked at the compliment. "Thanks," I replied.

Dad stepped close. "Why didn't you tell me you were seeing West Wainright before? He's worth billions."

I shrugged. "Because it's my personal life. Only mother cares about my dates."

"I do now that you're partner. Wainright's a good choice because of the money, but that's it. You can't be partner from Montana. I mean, I figured you'd give up by now and it wouldn't be an issue."

What?

Oh my God.

Give up by now.

It was so obvious now. My stomach dropped and I felt sick.

"Excuse me?" I cleared my throat because the words came out soft. "You... you never thought I'd get this far, did you?"

He frowned, but glanced away.

"You expected me to what, find a husband before now? You don't want me to have this partner spot at all, do you? Except I did everything you said, closed the final deal. You've been stringing me along."

He raised a hand. "I was wrong about that, Rory. I never thought you'd go through with it. Wanting to be a lawyer. You kept right on pushing. Your mother assured me you'd be sidetracked once you found a man."

"Are you fucking kidding me?"

He held up a hand to stop me. "You proved me wrong though."

"By finishing Columbia Law? By passing the bar on the first go? By interning for three years and working here for eight? By being your top biller? By being your best closer?"

"That's all good, but you didn't stand out."

"Didn't *stand out?*"

"Until Mike told me last week what you did with Wainright."

"What did I do with North?"

He frowned. "Not North. West. You slept with him. The patent holder himself."

My heart skittered, then started to beat double time. I popped to my feet.

"Mike told you that? And you believed him?"

"West was at the gala. He wouldn't have come unless you satisfied him."

Oh. My. God. *Oh my God.* Were my ears working?

I paced behind my desk trying to process his words. "So you gave me the partner job because I... used my body to full advantage? That I took one for the team?"

"Partners need to do anything for the firm," my father said. "And you did."

I faced him, set my hands on my hips. I was nauseated. Stunned. Freaked. This was my *dad.*

"You should have told me, Rory, about your strategy. I'm impressed. Proud even."

I stared at him. I knew my mouth hung open, but I couldn't close it.

My father was *proud* of me. Finally. Because I

supposedly fucked a client as a business strategy. Impressed enough to make me partner.

I looked at him. *Really* looked. He meant what he said. He wasn't stringing me along.

This office was mine. All I'd ever wanted. Except... not like this. I didn't want to be partner because Mike tattled. Or that my dad believed him, validated because West had been a nice guy to be at the gala for me.

I was repulsed that my father saw me having sex with a client as business strategy. That he held me in such low esteem that my sex life was a tool for him, not precious.

He also thought I was the kind of person to do it, that he actually rewarded such behavior.

What the fuck was wrong with him?

Nothing. God, he hadn't changed at all in the past few minutes. I had. I'd just had the last few pieces of the puzzle put into place. Or the last nail in the coffin of my career.

I told North I wanted the job in Montana. Even before I knew about all of this. I was done.

D.O.N.E.

I couldn't respect my father. I couldn't work beside him if he praised me for being a slut. God, he probably expected me to bill for the time as a *client meeting*, meaning I was worse than a slut. A prostitute. I'd told West this early on and I'd been right. So fucking right it hurt.

Instead of him praising my billable hour performance to his cronies going forward, he'd be telling them how I'd gotten the partner spot. The old-fashioned way for a woman. On her back.

Oh my God, Franklin had winked at me. No wonder.

I opened the bottom left drawer and grabbed my purse. I strode around the desk, paused long enough to say, "Dad, I quit."

Then left. Walked out of my life.

20

EST

WHEN I RETURNED from the stable for lunch, I froze when I saw East on my back porch. He was in my rocker, feet propped up on the rail, a glass of fucking iced tea in his hand.

"Make yourself at home," I grumbled, stalking up the steps.

"Don't mind if I do." He took a big gulp and made an exaggerated sigh. "You look thirsty. Have some tea."

I glared, stomped inside and poured myself a glass. Not because he told me too, but I was fucking thirsty.

I kicked the screen open and tossed my hat onto

the other chair. The one that nobody sat in because nobody ever came to the house. Except Rory.

She'd come.

Fuck, she'd *come.*

"Fucking hell," I muttered, then drank the whole glass in one go. "What are you doing here?"

"Right this second? Enjoying how miserable you are over a woman. Karma, brother."

I glared some more, set my glass on the railing. "Why would I be miserable about Rory? It was a fling."

His fair brow winged up. "You fly to New York for all your flings?"

I didn't reply. Why should I?

He didn't say a word, just drank some more of my tea.

"Rory wanted to be partner and now she is," I said finally, filling the silence.

"She did? That's great."

"Yeah. I'm not part of her life goals. I knew that going into her hotel room that day. I was fine with it that. I'm fine now."

Totally fine.

"You don't sound fine."

"I'm not fucking fine," I snapped. I paced down the length of the porch, then back. "You want to know how she earned the corner office?"

"Hard work?"

"Because a little shit told her father that she fucked me to close the deal."

East's jaw clenched. "That doesn't make sense. Shouldn't she be fired?"

I laughed. "No. She was promoted."

"I don't get it."

I ran a hand through my sweaty hair. "Right? Well, turns out, Daddy likes knowing his daughter had initiative. Was strategic enough to spread her legs for the patent holder. He likes that kind of can-do attitude."

"What the fuck? And she took the job?"

"She doesn't know."

He frowned. "What do you mean she doesn't know?"

"She's off on cloud nine thinking she earned the job because she's a fucking good lawyer. Meanwhile, I had to be part of a chat between that Spain fucker and Rory's father."

"A Spanish guy?"

I rolled my eyes. "No, the asshole's last name is Spain. He was vying with Rory for the promotion. Rory got it because her daddy was proud of her for her extra effort. Spain thought she'd be fired. You know what that's called?"

"Karma."

"Yeah."

I picked up my hat, dropped into the chair beside my brother.

"I hate knowing the truth. She deserves that spot. Free and clear. But while she's busting her ass for that company, they're thinking she'll fuck to close a deal."

"Then claim her. If she's only fucking you and no one else then–"

"She is only fucking me."

I hoped.

"Tell her."

"It's not my place. I'm a fling."

"If you were a fling, you wouldn't be so bent out of shape."

Dammit. He was right.

"Fine. I want more from her." I sighed. "You should have seen her the other night. So fucking pretty. That dress. Shit." I had to shift because my dick was getting hard.

"You're not moving to New York. You don't even leave the ranch."

I took a deep breath, gripped the arms of the chair. "Why does everyone keep saying that?"

"Because it's true."

"I leave the ranch."

"For food." East shifted in his seat. "I came here to talk to you about Tank Million and what we're going to do about him."

"Nothing," I replied quickly.

"See. There. That. You need to stop doing nothing."

"I went to New York!" I shouted, then grabbed his glass and finished it for him.

"And that means this woman means something to you."

"Tank Million means *nothing* to me," I countered.

East held up a hand. "I agree. But he wins if we do nothing."

"So we get to kill him?" The idea had me mentally rubbing my hands together in excitement.

"I wish. No. He went to the papers because we didn't pay him. He did it because he was pissed. A big fuck you to us."

"Now it's over. We can go back to our lives."

He leaned forward, set his forearms on his thighs. "What the fuck did that woman Cassie do to you?"

"Carrie."

"Whatever. This all goes back to that. You were at MIT and then you just quit. Came back, bought the ranch and never left."

"Because shit doesn't happen to me here."

"That's a boring as fuck life, brother. What did she do?"

"I loved her and she used me. Our name. The money. A job. She got everything she wanted out of me and then dumped me."

"So you quit college over that? Over a girl? How many guys go off to college, fall in love and get worked over by a chick? Every. Single. One. Including me."

I eyed him.

"Mara Seymour. Didn't love her, but I got wasted for two days because of her. Can't even smell tequila now without wanting to hurl."

"I didn't quit because of her. I quit because I was fucking bored. I had all these ideas." I pointed to my head. "MIT wasn't getting their hands on them and I didn't need any more classes."

"Okay, I can see that. But the rest? Jesus, you've been hiding here for years."

I looked down at my dusty boots. "You're the second person who's said that."

"Yeah, well, you're surrounded by smart people," he snapped. "Here's what's going to happen. We're going to meet with the PR team and you're going to put out a statement. Go on TV. Whatever they think is best."

"Me?"

"Where's Carrie now?" he asked.

I shrugged. "How the hell would I know?"

He pointed at me. "Exactly."

"She was like Macon. Using me. He laughed at everything I did. It's been safer to avoid," I admitted.

I stood, went to the railing and leaned against it. I stared out across my land. The sun was hot, the air still. It was a gorgeous day. Fuck, I loved it here.

But he was right. So was Rory. I'd been hiding.

"Macon's dead. You're the one who's been telling all of us to let that fucker rot. Carrie's probably on her third husband and caught VD from her personal assistant named Chet."

I couldn't help but smirk. That would be karma.

"You met Rory because of your patents So they're a good thing. Something to be proud of. *We're* proud of you."

"East," I groaned.

"We are, you fucker. It's time to show the world how awesome you are."

"Jesus, did you get that off an inspirational poster in the bathroom at school?"

He laughed.

"Rory thinks you're awesome."

"Rory thinks my dick is awesome."

He rolled his eyes and I grinned.

"If you're this caught up on Rory, dick skills or not, then you need to stop hiding. I'm not saying move to New York. Fuck, you'd be like that salsa commercial. But you need to be open to options. Including being with her."

"She called me on it," I admitted. "Saturday night. We argued."

"So maybe she only wants it to be a fling because you need to get past your issues first."

"Maybe." I had no fucking idea, actually.

Still, I nodded, then turned my head to look at my twin. "I can't solve Rory's problems unless she hands them to me to carry."

I wanted to be there for her. I'd proven it by flying to fucking New York. I'd left the gala with my balls empty but earlier than I thought. The pilot had needed to rest before he could legally fly again, so I'd slept on the airplane's couch until first light when we made the return trip. Rory would be at work now, probably in her new office, making deals and crushing men beneath her stiletto. Hopefully.

She hadn't texted. Neither had I.

"That's right," East replied. He'd been in love with Ella but she hadn't shared her issues with a former foster home kid until it was almost too late. "And you can't be there for her until you get off this ranch and go there, wherever the hell there is. Halfway, and I don't mean Wisconsin."

"But I can solve my problem. Ours. Tank's an asshole. Let's bury him."

His eyes brightened. "While I know you meant with the media, I still want to get a shovel."

21

ORY

AFTER THE REVELATION with my father, I went to my apartment, packed a suitcase and booked the first flight to Montana. Which put me in Atlanta for a four-hour layover, completely *not* in the right direction.

I wanted to go West.

No. I wanted *West.*

I missed him, even though we were completely wrong for each other. We had issues. Not sexually. But in every other aspect of our relationship.

No. We didn't have a *relationship.*

We had sex. And arguments.

Now I was headed to work for his sister. Was I crazy? Maybe. But that was better than being an idiot. Staying in New York would have been the stupidest thing ever. My mother had called five times. I'd get back to her. Eventually.

As I sat in an empty boarding area listening to airport recordings with a distinct Southern twang about suspicious packages, I realized that my clients were probably already assigned a different lawyer. My corner office was probably already claimed by Mike. Six projects had come in while I'd been in Montana. I hadn't been missed then.

I wouldn't be missed now. Or ever.

I wasn't anyone special to my father. Not in the office. Not in the family.

My mother wanted grandchildren. Maybe I'd give them to her someday, but she should be happy now that the partnership wasn't preventing the opportunity. And Matthew? He wouldn't even notice I left the state.

I had no idea what the hell I was doing. All I knew was that North was calling.

"You doing okay?" she said when I answered. I'd pretty much hung up on her and seven hours had passed.

I was alone in Georgia and I felt cared for with that

question. "I'm halfway to Montana," I replied. A woman pushing a stroller with a screaming toddler passed.

"Already? You move fast."

"There was no lingering. Once my mother hears I quit she'll be picking invitations with Mark Rutherford's mother."

"Who?"

"Do you really want to know?"

"You can tell me someday. Over wine."

She was the only one who knew I'd quit. Besides my father and probably the entire office. I wanted to tell West, that he'd been right about my job, my life. Everything. But I couldn't be sure he'd even answer my call. Or text.

"I'm freaking out a little, but I'm okay."

"Good. Tomorrow, after you finish your paperwork with HR, I've got your first project."

I took a deep breath. "Good. Work's good."

"Got your laptop with you?" she asked.

"You want me to work now?" I wondered even as I reached into my carry-on to pull it out.

"Once it's up, put this link in a browser," she said instead of answering.

I entered it and a page on the Wainright Holdings

website appeared. "Password?" I asked. I typed it in and a video came up.

"What's this about?"

"Tank Million."

"The man who said he was West's father?" I asked. "The one he met with when he took me to the airport?"

"Yes. On Saturday, Tank went to the press since we refused to give him any money."

Before the gala. He knew at the gala that Tank had outed his family.

"HR is giving this video to news outlets this afternoon."

"Should I watch?"

"Please."

Remembering I was in an airport, I grabbed my earbuds and stuck one in my ear. I held my cell up to the other.

I hit play.

It was West, standing on the front steps of North's house. The family house. Billionaire Ranch. I hadn't met his brothers, but I recognized them from photos. Beside each of them was, I assumed, the women they loved. North was there too, Jed standing slightly behind her.

He looked forward to whomever was shooting the

video.

"Hello. I'm West Wainright." He looked stiff and uncomfortable in front of the camera. He took a breath, his big chest expanding beneath his white button up shirt. I smiled at him, at his discomfort. This big, brawny guy was struggling.

"These are my siblings and family. As you are aware, Travis Million has gone to the media outlets about Macon Wainright. I'm sure you're expecting us to tell you he's a liar. We're not. I'm not. Because what he said was true. I think all of you can see from looking at me that I am Travis Million's son. But that doesn't mean we're family." West lifted his hand. "This is my family. They stand behind me... beside me."

He looked to East, who nodded.

"Macon Wainright was a gay man," West continued. "He kept that a secret from the world, including myself, East, South and North. We didn't know about this personal preference until after he died last year. Travis Million knew and was paid annually by Macon to keep quiet. To stay away from the Wainright family. He did, until last week, when he approached me and East for more money. We refused. His only outlet, his only source of revenge was to cause us damage through revealing this secret."

He paused, looked off in the distance past the

camera for a moment, then back at it. "It wasn't our secret he kept. We are not ashamed that Macon was gay. We are not ashamed of *anyone* who is gay. We are ashamed that Macon Wainright was a mean, abusive and controlling man. That he most likely hurt other people besides the four of us."

"Oh, West," I whispered.

"Most likely, including our mother," he continued. "She died when we were all very young, so we will never know her side of this story, but I will not have her memory tarnished by a man who only seeks revenge from this union, instead of a relationship with the children he made."

He cleared his throat, then tucked his hand in his jeans pocket.

"Travis Million may be my father, but he's no parent. He learned of us a few weeks ago. Instead of a relationship, he wanted money. That alone speaks to his character. I do not need to say anything further to tarnish it."

West spoke really well. Off the cuff but concise and... brilliant.

"The Wainright family will be contributing one hundred thousand dollars every year, the amount of money Macon paid Travis Million, to various charities for LGBTQ youth programs and to organizations that support abused women and children."

North reached out in the video and took his hand.

He offered the camera a small smile. "It will be better served to many in need, instead of to only one *in want.* Travis Million hopes you think there is a story here. There is none."

A tear fell onto the keyboard and I wiped it away.

"The man and I may share looks, but that is all. I will not hide."

The video ended and I looked around the boarding area, staring at nothing, seeing West. I pulled the earbud out. "Oh my God."

"He's pretty amazing, isn't he?" North asked.

I felt squishy inside. Like I wanted to go to West and hug him. To hold him. To tell him I was proud of him. Just as he'd done for me showing up at the gala.

"He's... wow," I admitted. "Are you okay? I mean, he's your dad too."

"Families are fucked up, aren't they?"

"Hell, yeah. I'm coming to Montana, aren't I?"

"Any fallout with *your* dad?"

"Like I said, I have messages from my mother. I haven't heard from my father, but I don't expect I will. I'm not sure exactly what to say anyway. I mean, he pretty much thinks I prostitute myself for the company's gain."

"Whatever you had... have... whatever tense you want to use, with West, isn't going to impact your job," she said. "Just because you used my brother for orgasms..."

I gasped in horror.

"Kidding."

I wasn't sure if she meant it or not. "Well, if you asked me when we first started talking about the patent contract that I'd turn down the partnership and come work for you, I'd have called you crazy. Now *I'm* the crazy one."

"Crazy in love with West."

I felt my cheeks heat and I was opening and closing my mouth like a guppy. "No. No. God no. Remember, orgasms only, right?"

She was quiet and I envisioned her squirming thinking about her brother having sex.

"I don't think he even wants to talk with me," I added. "I said some pretty strong things to him the other night."

"Maybe they were things he needed to hear."

I winced. "I accused him of hiding."

"Like he said in the video, he's not hiding now."

"He accused me of the same thing."

"You're not hiding now either," she replied. "Which means I need you to run legal for this issue."

"Does he even know I'm coming?"

"No, but he will soon enough. Your job tomorrow will be to work with PR to monitor any reaction from Tank or from anywhere else. Social media can be a nightmare."

"Sure."

"Great. Give me your flight information and I'll have someone pick you up."

"Um... are you sure after last time?"

She laughed. "No flings. I promise."

She knew everything that had happened. She wouldn't be that cruel.

"Fine." I pulled out my boarding pass and read her the flight info.

"North, do you think I did the right thing?" I asked her, having a moment of doubt.

"Take your father out of the scenario for a second. Would you keep working at a firm knowing your boss rewards you for having sex with clients to close deals?"

"Absolutely not." She didn't say anything. "Right. Okay."

"Everything's going to be fine. I know it. Just get here and it will all work out."

I wasn't so sure, but I wasn't chickening out now.

 EST

"YOU'RE NOT FUCKING with me again, are you?" I asked, turning my truck around.

"No. It's a new hire," North replied.

"Why do I have to pick him up?"

"Because South told me you were doing your food run."

"I didn't get to it last time I was in town," I explained, but she knew all too well the reason I'd never picked up any groceries from the mega-store. Rory.

"Right. So since you're there trying again…"

"Fine." I sighed. "Why doesn't he just take a cab to the hotel? I mean, can't people fend for themselves?"

"Seriously? Are you this much of an asshole? What kind of welcome is that?"

"Why aren't *you* picking this guy up?"

"You think Jed would let me?"

Jed would not let her pick up another guy from the airport and take him to a hotel. He wasn't jealous or worried North would cheat on him, but he was a possessive fucker. I didn't blame him. If my woman was— No. I had to stop my thoughts there because the vision of Rory came into my head.

Wrong. Totally wrong. She was married to her job. To the corner office.

I was the guy she'd cheated on that with. At least in her mind.

There would be no me and Rory.

"Fine," I grumbled. "Text me the flight info."

Two hours later, with coolers in the back of my truck full of perishable foods that would hold me for a month, I walked into the airport again. It had been a little over two weeks since the last time, since I'd met Rory and began our fling.

So much had happened. Our real father had entered our lives. And left them.

I was stronger. Better. I didn't think we were done

with Tank, but North had her PR team and lawyers taking care of any fallout. Since the video we shared had gone live, I was told there'd been lots of Internet chatter about the Wainrights. But I hadn't looked. I didn't care.

I wasn't hiding.

I chose to shrug it off. To let it go. Because Rory and everyone else had been right. I might be a big guy, but I'd been scared. Afraid to be hurt again.

I cut past the few counters of rental cars and made my way to baggage claim. The airport was busy, meaning a flight just landed. I had no idea who the guy was, but I figured it would be easy to spot another city slicker.

It was.

I froze and stared. Blinked.

"Rory?"

She spun around, her eyes widening.

Yeah, she hadn't been expecting me either.

North.

"What are you—"

"What are—"

We spoke over each other and I couldn't help but smile.

She wasn't wearing one of her power dresses today, but jeans and an untucked white blouse. Silver flip flops on her feet. I could see the hot pink polish on her toes. Her hair was pulled back in a sloppy knot on top of her head.

She looked... perfect.

"What are you doing here?" she asked as I stayed quiet, admittedly ogling her.

"North sent me to pick up the new hire. What are *you* doing here? And where's your phone?"

She raised her hand and waggled her fingers, showing me it wasn't in her hands. "I'm the new hire and my cell's in my purse because I have no emails. No briefs, torts, contracts. Nothing. I'm free."

If she'd said she was going on a mission to Mars I would have been less surprised.

"What?"

She glanced away. "Yeah, I... um, took a job with North this morning."

"Why? What—"

"I was right. Everyone thought I slept with you to close the deal."

I stepped closer, ran a hand over her jaw, cupped it.

"I know."

She frowned. "You do?"

I sighed. "At the gala, when you went to the ladies' room, your father and Mike had a little chat about how you got the job because you'd fucked me."

"Mike tattled, but I don't know how he knew."

"He didn't," I explained. "He was out to hurt you."

"It worked," she admitted.

I tugged her into my arms. Hugged her close and kissed the top of her head. "Kitten."

She sniffed, but when she looked up at me again, she hadn't been crying.

"It sucks. Not about Mike. He's always been a dick. But my dad... it's going to be a while for me to work my head around it."

I nodded because I was still tackling what Macon had done. I was better, all four of us were, but those scars lingered.

"Yeah. But kitten?" My thumb slid over her silky cheek. "I'll be here with you while you do."

"I'm not hiding any longer," she said.

I couldn't resist. I leaned down and kissed her. Soft and gentle. Savoring. Fuck, she was here.

"Me neither."

"I saw the video. I'm so proud of you."

"And I'm so proud of you. I wish I'd been there to witness your fury."

She rolled her eyes. "Not much fury."

"No balls crushed beneath your stiletto on the way out?"

"It's a waste of time. I have a life to live."

"That's right."

"Here, in Montana. I'm crazy."

"I'm crazy for you."

There, I admitted it.

Her eyes widened for a second and then she jumped up. Instinctively, I caught her. Then kissed the hell out of her.

Knowing we were in public, I broke the kiss before I ripped her shirt open and sucked on a nipple. "Where's your luggage? We need to find your luggage. Now."

Heat flared in her eyes. I slid her down my body so she knew her effect on me. Knew I was serious in the *now* part.

"There."

I recognized the case from her last trip and stalked over to snag it from the conveyor belt.

"This it?"

"I figure you need to take me to that seed and feed North mentioned for a new wardrobe."

"Later," she said.

I pulled up the handle on the suitcase.

"Walk or carry, kitten."

She frowned, then awareness bloomed in her eyes. "You can't think to—"

"Carry it is," I said, leaning forward and tossing

her over my shoulder.

"West!" she cried.

I couldn't help but grin as those waiting for their luggage watched. Rory was laughing so even the security guard didn't do anything.

I walked out of the building, towing her suitcase, my free arm wrapped around her thighs.

"I can walk," she said, once I'd cut across the crosswalk and to the parking lot.

"I've got something to fill that sassy mouth of yours."

She stilled, then squirmed. "Promise?"

I almost tripped over a curb at the one word. "Fuck," I breathed, then walked faster.

Because my truck was so big, I'd had to park at the back end of the lot. Thankfully, because I wasn't going to get us back to the ranch before I could get my hands on her. Hell, I wasn't going to get us out of the lot.

When we were by the truck, I let go of the suitcase and lowered Rory to her feet.

"Now, kitten. Gotta get my hands on you. Got to get you off."

She looked around as I opened the button on her jeans. There was no one nearby, only a few stragglers leaving from the incoming flight, but they all parked close to the building.

"Wait," she said.

My hand stilled before I slipped my fingers into her panties.

"I don't want a fling."

"Good. I don't want one either."

"What is this, West? What are we doing?"

I shrugged. "No idea. But I want you. Only you. I want to see where this goes. I want you with me. At the ranch. In my bed." I pulled my hand away and set it on my chest. "I think you might be here, too. Never done this before so I have no fucking clue."

She closed her eyes for a second, then looked up at me. "Me too. I took the job with North because I needed out. Away from that firm. From my job. From my family. Hell, New York. But I think I was running to you."

I took her mouth again. This time, not soft or gentle. Her tongue met mine.

When I lifted my head, our breathing was ragged. "I'll catch you, kitten. Always."

I touched her again, slid my fingers into her panties.

"We need to thank North," she said.

I arched a brow as I felt her wet heat. Fuck, she was always ready for me. "You want to talk about my sister while I'm fingering your pussy?"

"She did play matchmaker."

I laughed. "Yeah, she did. She'll never let us forget either."

"You going to talk or play with your pussy?" she dared.

My pussy.

I slipped a finger inside as she worked my belt buckle open, then my jeans. When she pulled me out and gripped the base, giving me one rough tug, I got busy.

Yeah, right there in the fucking parking lot, we got each other off. Because somehow, the wound tight New Yorker and the Montana rancher had found each other. And the only thing we'd do—hopefully forever —was to make each other happy. One orgasm at a time.

BONUS CONTENT

Guess what? I've got some bonus content for you! Sign up for my mailing list. There will be special bonus content for some of my books, just for my subscribers. Signing up will let you hear about my next release as soon as it is out, too (and you get a free book...wow!)

As always...thanks for loving my books and the wild ride!

Vanessa

JOIN THE WAGON TRAIN!

If you're on Facebook, please join my closed group, the Wagon Train! Don't miss out on the giveaways and hot cowboys!

https://www.facebook.com/ groups/vanessavalewagontrain/

GET A FREE BOOK!

Join my mailing list to be the first to know of new releases, free books, special prices and other author giveaways.

http://freeromanceread.com

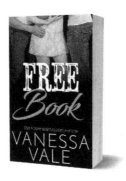

ABOUT VANESSA VALE

A USA Today bestseller, Vanessa Vale writes tempting romance with unapologetic bad boys who don't just fall in love, they fall hard. Her 75+ books have sold over one million copies. She lives in the American West where she's always finding inspiration for her next story. While she's not as skilled at social media as her kids, she loves to interact with readers.

Made in the USA
Columbia, SC
01 April 2022

58370602R00159